Cayman Cache

In for a Pound

Jeff Thompson

Papa T Books, LLC

Papa T Books, LLC

www.papatbooks.com

PRINTED IN THE UNITED STATES OF AMERICA

Dedicated to my family and all the adventures we have enjoyed. Also my friends who I have enjoyed many adventures with on land and sea.

Thank you to my friends who have been with me on this adventure and continue to provide support. Thanks to those for being part of the story and for encouragement and inspiration. Shawn Morgan and Richard James. Always appreciative of those who read the first draft and provide well needed critique and input, including Julia, and Anne. Here's to future adventures! Thanks also to my editor, Rob Thompson and another fantastic cover by Danna Mathias Steele.

Other works by the Author

Available at Amazon.com, Barnesandnoble.com
and papatbooks.com

Fiction

The Ian Marshall Series

Inlet Intrigue—The Trouble with Paradise (2022)
Exuma Escape—Chasing the Sun (2024)
Vegas Vendetta—All Bets Are Off (2024)

Children's Book Series

The Adventures of Mischief Macaw

Mischief Macaw Makes a Cake (2022)
Mischief Macaw Meets the Class (2022)
Mischief Macaw Makes a Friend (2023)
Mischief Macaw Meets Santa Claus (2023)
Mischief Macaw Makes the Team (2024)
Mischief Macaw Makes a Garden (2024)
Mischief Macaw Mows the Lawn (2024)
Mischief Macaw Makes a Volcano (2024)
Mischief Macaw Meets His Family (2024)
Mischief Macaw Misses School (2024)

Non-Fiction

Personal Finance for Life (2023)

Prologue

The dawn comes late as the wind howls across the water. The riggings come alive with an eerie hum whipped by the increasing breeze. "Secure the lines!" the captain shouts to his crew as they scurry about the deck, making ready for what's to come. The sky fades to dark gray. The winds gust, intermittently blowing spray from the white caps over the railing. The captain shouts orders to the crew and holds the ship as steady as he can with the choppy seas. He turns to the first mate and states, "She's a big one. Get everyone ready for the storm and make sure the cargo is secured. Clear the deck of anything that can be blown about."

"Aye, Captain, as you wish." And with that the first mate spins on his heel and begins to relay the captain's order to the rest of the crew.

The captain, tall, experienced and brave, has weathered storms over his many years at sea. He knows in his soul that this one is a beast and will require all his skill as a sailor, as well as a good bit of luck. The wind speed steadily increases each quarter hour. The rolling sea swells grow taller. He notices that the whitecaps are more frequent and increasing in size. "We'll make way toward the islands east of here and hope for the best. Maybe we can ride this out there," he yells out, hoping someone can hear him above the roar of the wind.

He manages to make way but the water currents driven by the wind are making progress slow. The *Nuestra Senora de Madeira* is battling the raging sea well, though. She's a good ship and has not let him down in his years as her captain.

Hours creep by and the captain is uncertain how they have stayed intact. He detects a small tear in the main sail that he knows will only grow larger, making his ship even more difficult to handle. He decides to keep her sails unfurled as he tries to make landfall on the islands.

Another hour passes. The tear in the main sail is now a large rip. The captain orders the crew to remain steadfast. The wind suddenly calms and the sea stills. It provides an incredible feeling of relief, but with a hint of dread. The sun is shining but all around on the horizon are ominous gray and black clouds. The captain, although confused at this horizon, is glad for a moment of calm.

"There's land, Captain, off our starboard. The islands for which we are aiming!" the first mate says as he peers through the eyeglass.

"We'll continue to make way for those islands," says the captain. "We'll take inventory and check for damages, as well as make necessary repairs." He points the ship in the direction of the islands he can see in the distance.

Half an hour later, he isn't making much progress but he decides to stay the course. Suddenly, the island disappears into clouds and the unending wall moves straight for them. He doesn't realize they are in the eye of the hurricane, and they're only halfway through the storm. In what seems like seconds, they are engulfed in the back side of the storm, heading the ship for a small island in the middle of the ocean. The wind is more intense and blowing in the opposite direction as they were before the calm. The sails don't stand a chance. They become tattered and virtually useless. The captain maintains the course he hopes will lead to land.

Wham! A shallow reef below the surface doesn't budge. *The Nuestra Senora de Madeira* is firmly wedged on the rocks. As the wind continues its fury and the waves continue to pound the now helpless vessel, the ship rips apart. The crew of thirty is scattered about.

The captain runs to his cabin to retrieve his personal cache. He opens a small crate and grabs the one item that must not be lost, as well as his diary, both wrapped in seal skin. He tucks them under his arm and runs for the railing.

Another huge wave washes the ship over the reef and scatters the wreck across two thousand feet of ocean.

Coral, sand and debris stir up from the storm, which envelop the wreckage now strewn across the reef and beyond. The captain, the first mate and half of the remaining crewmen are lost.

The *Nuestra Senora de Madeira* has been shattered. Part of a 1730 Spanish treasure fleet, the ship's cargo is scattered across nearly a mile of ocean bottom as the storm subsides. The captain sees his box full of emeralds, ranging in size from two to twenty-five carats, as the container flies open and sinks with the rest of the debris. The hammered-gold chalice with the single ruby he put inside his coat remains there and will rest with him in his watery grave, his diary floating on the whitecaps.

In his logbook, the captain details how they were a simple merchant ship making for Spain from Havana in 1730. The cargo is listed as molasses, sugar cane, rum and some armaments. What the logbook fails to mention is detailed in the captain's diary. The one hundred thousand gold doubloons and two hundred thousand silver coins, along with emeralds and other precious stones. The logbook also does not detail that the captain had been delayed in his departure due to a storm in the Florida Straits, and that he instead tried to sail south around the tip of Cuba in an attempt to join the rest of the fleet. The captain had sworn an oath to not reveal to anyone what he was carrying, or the significance of the chalice. His charge had been to deliver the ship to the Port of Seville, a river port in Spain, located on the lower reaches of the Guadalquivir, in the city of Seville. He was to arrive approximately one month after departing Havana. Now, the only one who knows what is really on the ship is the ocean herself.

Chapter 1

The wedding is simple yet elegant and practically perfect. Emma looks absolutely stunning in her antique white bridal gown accented with lace and pearls sewn intricately into the lace. The gown is silk and sleek and so very Emma. Alistair is properly attired in his very formal tuxedo, black tails with white gloves, a top hat and a black-and-gray ascot. Emma has a sister, Gail, who serves as her maid of honor. Gail is bedecked in a similar dress to the bride, except the color is a very rich silver-gray. Alistair has David Smith as his best man. David wears full military dress complete with the medals, epaulets and insignia of the British special forces. David is slightly taller than Alistair and sports blondish gray hair, which sneaks out from under his military hat. The ceremony is conducted by the vicar of the Church of England St. Andrew's Chapel in Colchester. It is one of the oldest churches in

Colchester, having served the people of Greenstead since the 11th century.

A lovely ceremony using traditional vows, with Alistair and Emma pledging their love and commitment to each other. After a brief explanation of roles, and blessings by the vicar, they exchange rings and the light the unity candle.

The entire crew associated with the fusion reactor, its development and continued protection are in full attendance. There is Alistair's team of George, Aiden and Ethan. Shawn and Sandra are there, as is Ian, who is accompanied by Dawson, still using her assumed identity, Hannah Flynn, given to her for witness-protection purposes after the Vegas operation in the previous year. David Smith has his latest team of covert operators in full dress. There are a few others that Alistair has invited but were not associated with his team of brilliant scientists and brave partners who are always at the right place at the right time. Richard Branson sent his regrets as he is off on another adventure and simply could not get back in time from the Himalayas.

Peter, Alistair's personal chef, is invited to attend the wedding along with his sous chef, Emily, but he insists that they prefer to do the preparation and cooking for the reception after the ceremony. "It would be my honor to serve you and your guests on this very special day," Peter tells Alistair. "I will prepare your favorites, as well as anything special that your bride-to-be, Ms. Greene, would like. Oh, and I do need to speak to her about her cake of choice!" Alistair knows that he will not win the argument to have the affair catered so he relents and provides a menu for Peter and Emily to prepare.

The cake is a traditional Great British Wedding Cake with three tiers. A twelve-inch base, a nine-inch middle tier and a six-inch top tier. Fondant roses adorn each of the tiers, which are all iced white with a delicious icing that includes apricot jam and marzipan. The decorative roses are a soft pink. The cake itself is made of raisins, sultanas, orange zest, black treacle, cloves and ginger in addition to the traditional cake ingredients.

Emma couldn't have been happier with the way the cake is presented. She is equally thrilled with the menu of a traditional English reception that nearly mirrors the menu for Prince William and Kate Middleton's celebration. The starter course includes marinated South Uist salmon and Lyme Bay crab. The main course, Saddle of North Highland Mey select organic lamb, is served with Highgrove spring vegetables, English asparagus, Jersey Royal potatoes, and Sauce Windsor. And for dessert, the couple enjoy a trio of Berkshire honey ice cream.

After the reception and a full evening of recounting stories from their adventures over the past several years, the group once again says their goodbyes. No tears, though. Hearty hugs and handshakes and wishes for success. The English scientists are busy building and perfecting their floating platforms and designing floating neighborhoods utilizing the power and water production from the fusion device they have designed, built and are now adapting for other uses. Alistair James and his scientific team, consisting of Emma, Ethan, Aiden, George, and the late Benjamin Burns, have been able to develop and employ a small nuclear fusion device that not only provides eco-friendly power, but also clean water as a by-product. It runs solely on seawater. The device has been central to many of the adventures over the past several of years.

Ian and Alistair share a private moment off to the side from the others. "I'll never be able to thank you for all you've done for me, Alistair." Ian speaks with a slight catch in his voice. "I do have one request."

"None of this would have been possible without your efforts, Ian. What is your request?"

"Can we come up with a name for the fusion device? I mean, we just keep calling it 'the device'," Ian says.

"I guess we hadn't thought of that. We'll have to put some thought to it," Alistair replies.

"Shawn, Aiden and I were thinking that an appropriate name might be the Ben Burns Power Station," Ian offers.

"Brilliant. In honor of our departed colleague and collaborator, Benjamin Burns. Okay, that's what we'll call it from now on!"

They shake hands and return to the reception to join the others.

Chapter 2

The Treasure of Lima is a legendary treasure reputedly removed from Lima, Peru in 1820 and never recovered. It is estimated to be worth somewhere between two hundred and four hundred million dollars in today's money. Some estimates have the value up to one billion dollars.

Spain controlled Lima from the sixteenth century when it defeated the Incas. In the centuries that followed, the Roman Catholic Church gathered a huge treasure in Lima. In the early nineteenth century, Spain began to have difficulties with its colonies due to wars of independence in South America. Lima was no exception and, in 1820, the city came under heavy pressure and finally had to be evacuated.

Lima was on the edge of revolt. As a preventative measure, the Viceroy of Lima decided to transport the city's fabulous wealth to Mexico for safekeeping.

The treasures included jeweled stones, candlesticks and a life-size solid-gold statue of Mary holding the baby Jesus.

Captain William Thompson, commander of the *Mary Dear,* was put in charge of transporting the riches to Mexico. Thompson and his crew proved to be unable to resist the temptation; they turned pirate, cut the throats of the guards and accompanying priests, and threw their bodies overboard.

Thompson headed for Cocos Island, off the coast of Costa Rica, where he and his men allegedly buried the treasure. They then decided to split up and lay low until the situation had calmed down, at which time they would reconvene to divvy up the spoils.

However, the *Mary Dear* was captured, and the crew went on trial for piracy. All but Thompson and his first mate, James Alexander Forbes, were hanged. To save their lives, the two agreed to lead the Spanish to the stolen treasure. They took them as far as Cocos Island and then managed to escape into the jungle. Thompson and Forbes fled the island and the treasure was never seen again.

As the story goes, they made their separate ways—Thompson to Newfoundland and Forbes to California, where he became a successful businessman—but never returned to the island.

The *Mary Dear* never yielded the motherlode that she was purported to be carrying. The ship never gave up the secret of the treasure.

Chapter 3

Shawn and Sandra fly back to Peter Island to tend to the small inn Sandra purchased a short while ago. Ian and Hannah are flying there as well to pick up the *Second Wind* and prepare for their next sail to another part of the Caribbean.

A few hours before their flight departs Heathrow, Shawn receives a phone call from a friend he has not heard from in many years. "Jackson" flashes as the incoming caller. Shawn excuses himself from the others and take the call.

"Shawn!" Jackson shouts. "How are you, my friend?"

"Jackson Collins, how many years has it been? You still trying to find the next motherlode from whatever treasure trove you're chasing?" Shawn responds.

"Very funny. When I find it, I'll make sure you're the second to know so I can rub your nose it in! Or, if you'd like to get in on the discovery with me, you could come help me with a little bit of research, do some scouting, and maybe help me haul in the next great discovery!"

"I'm heading back to the British Virgin Islands within the hour. But tell me where you're at and where you think this mysterious treasure is located," Shawn says. "I'll roam about in cyberspace and see what possibilities abound."

"Text me when you get home and I'll send you the necessary details. I don't want to discuss this over the phone, just in case I'm right." Jackson laughs.

"Okay, Mr. Cautious. I'll give you a call tomorrow."

The next day on Peter Island, Sandra is busy catching up with the inn and what details need tending to from the short time she was away. Shawn decides to contact Jackson and let him know he's back.

Not long after the text, Jackson sends an encrypted email to Shawn containing his location, the location of the suspected treasure, and the ship he's trying to find. He studies the information contained in Jackson's email in detail. He does initial research into the claims of what the ship was carrying and where she supposedly went down. He is confused about some of the details but his interest is piqued with curiosity. Shawn figures that he can spare a few weeks to help Jackson while Sandra gets the affairs of her inn in order and ready for the upcoming tourist season.

Shawn asks Ian, "Are you interested in going with me and possibly discovering some long-lost treasure?"

"I'm good, my friend. I'm off on the *Second Wind* with Hannah to do a little exploration," Ian replies.

The *Second Wind* is a Viking 48 convertible—a gift from Alistair for all their help in getting the Ben Burns Power Station up and running. "Plus, I told

Alistair that I'd check up on the Ben Burns Power Station models that were operating on Jost Van Dyke and Necker Island, along with a few of the others that are deployed in the area," Ian explains. "As a bonus, I have this beautiful redheaded first mate that loves to go topless while we're sailing."

Shawn laughs. "Okay then, you be safe out there. We'll catch up soon!"

After spending a few days getting unpacked and repacked, he makes arrangements to meet Jackson on Cayman Brac, one of the three islands in the Cayman Island chain. He kisses Sandra goodbye and leaves for Beef Island and the airport on Tortola.

Getting from one small island airport to another small island airport is a surprisingly easy task. Simpler than Shawn thought. The American Airlines flight from Terrance B. Lettsome International in Tortola to Miami is only two hours with the time change. Similarly, the flight from Miami to Owen Roberts International on Grand Cayman is less than one hour. Then a short hop to Gerrard Smith International Airport on Cayman Brac via Cayman Airways. But there is one catch. His layover in Miami is just under fifteen hours. Having no checked baggage, he has no desire to stay in the airport, or Miami itself, for that many hours. He decides to rent a car and drive to Islamorada in the Florida Keys. He gets his rental, a Jeep Wrangler ragtop, one of popular rental cars of the Keys. It is a hideous yellow but it is fine for the short time he will be there. Seventy-four miles from the airport to the Moorings for a short stay.

The Moorings Village is home to a private, spacious beachfront resort that provides a natural social-distancing environment and atmosphere. Tropical, tranquil and untouched, the former coconut plantation boasts coconut palms, numerous orchid varieties and eight private cottages tucked into the lushly landscaped estate. There is even a private production studio available for photo and video shoots for commercials and movie backdrops. In fact, the Netflix series *Bloodline* was filmed there and around Islamorada. It is barefoot luxury. Shawn decides to treat himself. He loves the Moorings, and besides, he is unsure the accommodations Jackson may have secured in the Caymans. "I hope it has walls and a roof," Shawn thinks to himself.

On the drive down US 1, he can't decide between Marker 88, Lor-e-lei's, or Ziggie & Mad Dog's for dinner. He hasn't eaten since breakfast and it will be mid-evening before he sits at a table. He opts for the phyllo-encrusted escargot and the stuffed yellow tail snapper at Ziggie & Mad Dog's, paired with a nice Stags' Leap Investor Napa Valley red.

After the fantastic dinner and a fitful night's sleep, he jumps in the lemon-colored Jeep and returns up US 1 North to Miami. It seems in no time his Cayman Airways flight to Cayman Brac is on the ground and he heads for the terminal. The sun beats down on the tarmac, giving a mirage of silvery water puddles in the late-morning sunshine.

Jackson is there to bear hug him when he gets inside. "Great to see you, Shawn! Been too long."

"Great to see you, Jackson! I'm looking forward to getting caught up with you and everything that's been going on since our last get together." By that, he meant the last time he and Jackson were in harm's way. Shawn and Jackson are former members of a secret task force. For many years, they worked all over the world protecting unknowing citizens and putting away really bad people. The sphere of their operation was primarily in the western hemisphere. Jackson, who is a few years older than Shawn, retired earlier. Shawn just entered retirement this past year.

Jackson explains to Shawn that he found a tattered map in an old Bible. The map has verse written on it. The Bible is in the name of James Alexander Forbes, penned on the page before Genesis. Jackson believes it's a map to the Treasure of Lima. Shawn tells him, "That treasure was buried on Cocos Island.

It's nowhere near the Caymans. In fact, Cocos Island is in the Pacific."

Cocos Island is of volcanic origin, lying in the Pacific Ocean about three hundred miles south of the Osa Peninsula, Costa Rica. It rises to an elevation of approximately two thousand eight hundred feet above sea level, is about five miles long and three miles wide, and has a total area of nine square miles. Geologically, it is part of the Cocos Ridge and is related to the Galapagos Islands to the south. Similar to the Galapagos, Cocos Island, because of the distance from the mainland, is an important repository of species unique to the island. In 1982, it was designated Cocos Island National Park.

The rugged, uninhabited island has two natural harbors, Wafer Bay and Chatham Bay, both located on the north coast. Cocos gained notoriety during the colonial era as a haven for pirates and as an alleged site of their buried treasures, which have never been found, despite the attempts of hundreds of expeditions.

"On the contrary! What if that's what they want everyone to believe? They want everyone to think that they buried the treasure on an island lying three hundred and forty miles off the Pacific coast of Costa Rica. There have been how many expeditions and nobody has found anything of consequence? So, my question to you is, what if the Treasure of Lima wasn't even on the *Mary Dear* when they got to Cocos Island?"

"What the hell are you saying?" Shawn excitedly speaks up. "You telling me that they left Lima laden with up to a billion dollars in treasure but it magically disappeared?"

"Not disappeared. Rerouted! Thompson and Forbes had ten trusted confidants who were with them for many years. Even in the cutthroat world of piracy, a few were bound by loyalty and trust in their captain. The treasure was loaded at Lima.

Thompson and Forbes and their men sailed for Mexico along with some priests and the priests assistants who tended the treasure and who were not in on the plan. But after a hundred miles of sailing in that direction, they killed and tossed the others overboard and looped back, only to land at Puerto Quimba near La Palma in Panama.

From there, they hired a small but hearty group of natives, who led them across the lower part of Panama along the rivers until they reached the mountains. The crossing was long and arduous but they made it with no loss of life and made Mosquito Point, or Punta Mosquito. Their laborers were paid handsomely, not only for their work, but also their solemn vow of silence. They were able to purchase a small but stout vessel with some of the gold from the treasure and began the loading process on their own. In total, the excursion took the better part of a month. The trek with regards to elevation was not extreme. They loaded the treasure in wagons and on pack animals at sea level. The highest elevation they reached was just above two thousand feet along the coastal mountain ranges before descending toward the Atlantic. Most of the journey took them through mixed evergreen and deciduous forests with occasional scrub areas in central Panama. The final part of the journey was the most difficult. Crossing the low-level mountain ranges. Their guide chose the path between the Serrania del Darien and the Serrania de San Blas, the mountain ranges on the southern Atlantic coast. After the descent, they found themselves at Punta Mosquito.

In the meantime, Thompson and Forbes sail the *Mary Dear* with the remainder of their crew on to Cocos Island. Basically, leading the Spanish on a wild goose chase to find the treasure on Cocos. Once there, he and Forbes disappear into the jungle. Through a series of bribes and detours, along with being stowaways and, later, deckhands on a vessel, they make their way to the Atlantic side of Panama and rejoin their loyal crewmen. They load the treasure and sail north, hoping to make it to the

United States and into Savannah Harbor. They would determine how and where to store, divide and sell their treasure. However, sailing even the small vessel was terribly difficult, made even more so with the weight of the gold and silver.

They ran into a terrible storm. Unbeknownst to them, a category-four hurricane engulfed the ship and they tried to make it to what is known Cayman Brac. They failed when they struck a reef, and both men and crew were thrown into the sea. The loyal crewmen who remained with Thompson were lost. Thompson and Forbes floated on some ship's wreckage to Cayman Brac.

After a few weeks, they ventured out on a small boat they had borrowed from one of the locals who had befriended them. They dove the shallow part of the reef and retrieved a relatively small amount of coins and jewels. The ocean had already been covered much of the treasure with sand, silt and rock from the devastating storm. Further shifting from the currents in the few weeks since the wreck meant that, without proper salvage equipment, the motherlode was lost. It was at this point that Thompson and Forbes went their separate ways."

"That's quite the tale, my friend. A fantastic story, but what are you basing this potential reroute of the treasure on? What facts have you found? Are you sure you haven't been sipping rum in the sun too long?" Shawn laughs.

"Okay, and what do you make of this?" Jackson quickly replies.

Shawn reads the verse. According to the verse found in Forbes' Bible, what Jackson has been saying would, in fact, be true. "Why in the world would anyone go to those lengths and in those conditions of the day to move the treasure across the Isthmus of Panama." Shawn asks, puzzled.

"I might have the answer. Let me show you this. It's the deathbed confession of one John Keating. He is an alleged acquaintance of Thompson. I haven't confirmed it but I believe he is one of the original ten sailors that moved the treasure across Panama. He contracted malaria and died in Panama. I found this letter in a dusty, forgotten corner cabinet in the archives in Panama. Here's what he says was in Thompson and Forbes' possession."

Jackson hands Shawn an old letter, yellowed from age and the ink fading. John Keating recalls his connection to Thompson. Upon Keating's deathbed, he wrote the following inventory.

*One chest containing altar trimmings of gold cloth with canopies, monstrances, chalices all coated with gemstones of up to one thousand two hundred and forty-four pieces.

*One chest with two gold relic containers weighing one hundred twenty pounds with six hundred twenty-four topaz, carnelians, emeralds and twelve diamonds.

*One chest containing three relic containers of cast metal weighing one hundred sixty pounds with eight hundred sixty rubies, nineteen diamonds and other gemstones.

*One chest containing four thousand doubloons of Spanish Marked Eight, one hundred twenty four swords, five thousand crowns of Mexican gold, sixty-four daggers, one hundred twenty shoulder belts and twenty-eight round shields.

*One chest containing eight caskets of cedar wood and silver with three thousand eight hundred forty cut stones, rings offering plates and four thousand two hundred sixty-five uncut stones.

*Seven chests with twenty-two candelabra in gold and silver weighing two hundred fifty pounds and one hundred sixty-four rubies.

*One seven-foot solid-gold statue of Virgin Mary with Baby Jesus. Weighing seven hundred eighty pounds, rolled on her gold chasuble adorned with one thousand six hundred eighty-four jewels including four-inch emeralds, six-inch topazes and seven crosses made of diamonds.

"That's why they planned and carried out such an elaborate and complicated scheme. The treasure is immense in terms of what it included. The statue of the Virgin Mary with Baby Jesus is priceless. Now, if it's true that it exists, where is it resting? Is it covered up by the sea or has it been recovered and transformed to more easily tradeable gold pieces? We're not going to know until we dive and see if we can find any of the Thompson and Forbes treasure," Jackson concludes.

Shawn tells him he's more than intrigued but, before they bring in some serious treasure-hunting boats and equipment, they need to find some proof that the treasure does still exist and that it exists not off Costa Rica, but off of Cayman Brac.

More than three hundred and twenty-five ships sank around the Cayman Islands, which lay in the path of sailing vessels plying between Spain, the Spanish territories and Cuba, the last stop before setting out on the open sea for Europe. Over the years, amateur and professional divers have discovered a substantial amount of sunken treasure in the area but no motherlodes. Only the occasional gold coin or small gold chain or pieces of eight.

"All right, my interest is definitely piqued," Shawn replies. "You mentioned research. Tell me about the research. What have you found?"

"The name of the ship they sailed out of Panama on was a smallish but stout Spanish galleon, *La Senora de Colon*. It was only eighty feet in length with three masts. Most galleons were one hundred feet or more with up to four masts. Thompson sailed with his first mate Forbes, the ten crewman and a handful of willing crew that assisted in their overland trek. They had been assisted in the loading and planning of the sailing route by a handful of native Panamanians, who helped them greatly with the movement of the treasure across Panama. They then loaded *La Senora de Colon*. Obviously, it would be immensely helpful to find a ship's bell or a cannon or something that would identify her as the Colon. Here. I was able to get the schematic and other specifics of the ship when I went to Panama City last year," Jackson says as he hands Shawn the documents.

"That's terrific," Shawn gets a word in. "At least we know what we're looking for."

"In going through the archives at several museums, as well as several churches along the suspected path across the Panamanian Isthmus, I found and made copies of accounts of a trek that has eerily similar characteristics to my theory." He hands Shawn a large leather binder.

"Again, that's outstanding. It would be nice if one of those accounts mentioned the *Mary Drear*, the Virgin Mary statue or anything specific to that treasure," Shawn says.

"I've got more. I went to the General Archive of the Indies, housed in the ancient merchants' exchange of Seville, the Casa Lonja de Mercaderes. It's the repository of extremely valuable archival documents illustrating the history of the Spanish Empire in the Americas and Asia," Jackson continues. "I tried to get permission to visit Havana to comb their archives but I was denied any access."

"We're off to a good start then. We need to look at the currents along the area where we think the ship went down. Estimates of overburden will be crucial to determine how far under the sand we might need to look. I'll make contact with some friends at NOAA. I'll also try to determine how the debris may have shifted over time. Once we have all the information we can muster, gather some of the vital exploration equipment, then we'll get into the water and do some exploring."

"That's the ultimate goal, of course. The research and the planning is critical. We need to get some solid hits from our scanning equipment, but we're not going to find anything without getting down there and moving some sand," Jackson concurs.

Chapter 4

There are several nations that sponsor terrorism in the world. The United States, United Kingdom, Europe and much of the free world keep tabs on them and spend vast amounts of resources making sure that they do not develop nuclear capability, while continuing to pursue compromise through diplomacy rather than force. It is the countries, and even factions within those countries, that fly under the radar who are the true threat. Those wanting to be next in line to create and breed chaos are the real worry. Take a group of dedicated radicals with a powerful leader, give them connections, money and resources. You then have an unknown but formidable enemy.

One such militant group has been established on the island nation of Haiti. They are poorly financed but they are bound by their loyalty to each other and the cause to free their country from poverty. The leader of the group, *Libérer Haiti,* is Jean Pierre. He is a rugged native from near Belladere in the mountains near the Dominican border. Jean is of French and Creole decent. He is taller than average for a Haitian, standing five feet ten inches and carries a fit physique. The Belladere region is a rural area where coffee farmers struggle with poverty and environmental challenges. Jean has lost family due to the impoverished conditions in which they are forced to live. He is determined that, one day, he will have a positive impact on the people by any means necessary. The Haitian government and its officials are no help, as they are more concerned with not being executed during the next coup attempt and with lining their pockets with aid money meant for the populace.

Jean Pierre has learned to read people. He is self-educated for the most part, only attending school infrequently as a youth. He is an avid reader and absorbs any and all information he can lay his hands on. He has several close friends and a few confidants.

His name is being mentioned in small circles in the area and gaining some notice. He does not steal and is not a criminal. He will not take from his own people.

He has intentionally become more and more political in his views. He becomes more radical and talks to his friends about the changes that he believes should be made. They used to meet in homes until the attendance became large enough to move them outside, where the crowds now seem to grow with each gathering. Over the period of five years, Jean Pierre went from a disgruntled youth to a leader—a voice for his people. But the powers that determine the politics in Haiti do not support him. At this rate, he will go no farther than being a low-level voice of the people. He decides he must take another route to achieve his goal of becoming a factor for change. He will need to find another way to get his voice heard outside of his homeland.

Jean Pierre has a group of about thirty followers who are truly loyal to him. One of them, Paul Baptiste, approaches him one day and tells him, "We need to make a statement. We need to force the government to listen."

"I realize that," Jean Pierre replies, "but how are we going to do that."

"We kidnap a leader. We collect ransom for their release," Paul explains.

"Kidnapping and ransom?!" Jean shouts back. "Who, what, where? We will likely receive unwanted retribution for such an act. No, I think we need to come up with another solution."

"Military coup? Government overthrow?"

"We simply don't have the manpower or backing. Let's continue to think through the process and work on developing a solid endgame that has the possibility of some success."

Unbeknownst to Jean Pierre, there is a Cuban national with blessings from the leaders in Havana who constantly seeks opportunities to fund and organize rebel groups in the Caribbean. He has gotten wind of this ragtag *Libérer Haiti*.

The Cuban's directive from Havana is to make contacts, obtain commitment from these rebel groups and help them achieve funding. The objective being that these rebel factions will be loyal to Cuba and overthrow governments, giving Cuba a firmer foothold in the area. Cuba, however, has an economy that is suffering from decades of neglect and governmental control. Antonio Morales will need to find funding and resources on his own. His government has none to spare.

In addition to garnishing favor with the rebel groups he has recruited, his calling card has been to create mayhem and chaos. He particularly despises the capitalists and their presence in the Caribbean.

Antonio Morales' limited financial resources leads him to develop an explosive device capable of damaging the infrastructure of an industry, crippling an unstable nation. The sheer threat of a bombing, in some cases, will bring forth offers of cash or other remediation.

Morales is a dedicated soldier in the war against capitalism. He has been a loyal soldier for his country. But he is growing weary of his own government. Then there are the Russian, and now the Chinese, influencers knocking on the political doors in Havana and handing out cash to allow these countries to gain a foothold in the region and spy on the United States.

Morales is paid through the Cuban government, working as a research and development officer. His cover is to develop plans to help the Cuban people. However, his real purpose is more nefarious.

He is based out of Havana but has recently set up a small warehouse in the city of Puerto Padre in the

Las Tunas province of Cuba. It is located on the northern coastal region of the province, in an estuary that opens into the Puerto Padre Bay, very close to the western side of Hispaniola.

Known popularly as the City of Mills, Puerto Padre has a history dating back to the sixteenth century. In the mid-nineteenth century, the city began its transformation from a small town into an industrial center with the construction of its first sugarcane mill. The town played a large role in Cuba's wars of independence, and today is something of a tourist center. The founders were Creole landowners of Castilian ancestry and Catalan merchants.

At least two rivers lead into Puerto Padre Bay. The small islet of Cayo Juan Claro is located toward the eastern center side of the bay; the Puerto Carupano port is located in this islet, which is connected to the mainland by a manmade road. A railroad connects the islet with the now defunct sugar factory in the nearby town of Delicias. The terrain is mainly formed of flatland, although the city itself sits on a small hill, which rolls nicely into the sea. The immediate terrain nearby the town is swampy with a thick mangrove forest.

Morales is very fond of the location. He's very close to Guantanamo Bay, where the American military maintains a base, even though they are not a welcome guest. He's very near the Bahamas and the southern tip of Florida should he need to pay those spots a visit.

He sends word to a Haiti contact that he wants to meet with: one Jean Pierre. Antonio wants to offer Jean Pierre an opportunity to lead a rebellion that will not only profit him financially but also in stature and will help fuel his cause.

Through a series of phone calls and verbal communications, word finally reaches Jean Pierre. Antonio's original plan is to have a small private plane fly into Belladere airfield. It is a small airport that is not well maintained. Morales, in making arrangements for the flight, discovers through satellite images that the airport is closed due to structures encroaching the eastern end of the runway. Rather than selecting another small airport in the region, the most direct route is to fly into and out of Toussaint Louverture International Airport in the bustling capital of Port-au-Prince.

Jean Pierre will then fly to Hermanos Ameijeiras Airport, which services the Las Tunas Province in Cuba and is the nearest airport to the warehouse Morales has set up in Puerto Padre. Jean and Antonio will meet to size each other up and determine if and when the two can come to a working agreement on the future of *Libérer Haiti*.

Chapter 5

Ian and Hannah sail to check on the units on a few of the islands. Foxy Caldwell completes his research into helping some of the other islands by selecting trusted islanders to carry out and maintain the units.

There are units on Jost Van Dyke, Anegada, Peter Island, Virgin Gorda and two on Tortola in the BVI. There is also one in St. John, one in St. Croix and one in St. Thomas.

Foxy has reached out and is seeking some guidance to place units in St. Kitts, Dominica and Tobago. He also is checking with an old friend in the sparsely populated Acklins and Crooked Islands in the Bahamas archipelago from many years back. John "Bonefisher" Campbell is his long-time friend, as well as an expert bonefishing guide. He is the unofficial mayor of the Acklins, and enjoys a status much like Foxy's standing on Jost Van Dyke.

Acklins is one of a group of islands arranged along a large, shallow lagoon called the Bight of Acklins. The Bight is home to one of the best bonefishing areas in the region. The area has a population of only about six hundred people. It is ideal for a test location in the lesser developed and needy area of the island chain.

John is more than eager about the prospect and asks when he can get started with this Ben Burns Power Plant. "Soon, my friend," Foxy tells him. I have a unit I can ship to you in a few weeks and I'll come there and get you up and running."

"That sounds great, Foxy," John replies. "It will be a huge benefit to the people of the island."

Foxy tells John what he needs to get ready for the new unit. He asks him to find a couple of locations near but not on the beach. Also he tells John he will need to build a small shelter or shed to house the unit and protect it from the elements and, perhaps, prying eyes.

"I'll get on it right away," John says enthusiastically.

After a few weeks go by. Foxy accompanies the unit to the Acklins aboard a seaplane that Alistair has kept in Nassau. Since Alistair sold Cat Cay and it is under development as a new island resort for the rich and famous, Foxy told Alistair that he could fly the unit from St. Thomas to Nassau and boat it to Acklins Island.

Alistair said, "Nonsense. I'll arrange for a pilot to fly the plane to St. Thomas. Then you move one of the units still in storage there and he can fly you from St. Thomas to Acklins. I'll have him put the floats on the plane so you can easily land it in the water."

The plane is a Cessna 208 Caravan. It is excellent for carrying people or cargo and has a range of over one thousand, two hundred miles. The Cessna 208 is a high-wing, braced-cabin monoplane powered by a single Pratt & Whitney turboprop. Alistair's model has the adaptation of floats with retractable landing gear, this giving him the option of using either the runway or the water for takeoff and landing.

Foxy inspects the set-up John has completed and is very pleased. He and John gather a small crew of trusted islanders to assist in the setup. In a few hours, Foxy has the unit up and running. Power is being supplied to Lovely Bay Settlement on the north side and it is housed on the property that houses Acklins' Creekside Bonefish Lodge.

Foxy tells John, "You will be amazed with the unit. You will have endless power and clean water for drinking and for irrigation. I'm telling you as an experienced beneficiary of a unit. It's just amazing and incredibly beneficial. I still don't believe it."

"I can't tell you how much I appreciate this, Foxy," John says.

"My pleasure, my friend. Do be mindful that people have gone to great lengths to try to steal one of these units and have failed. There have even been attempts at sabotage. The Ben Burns Power Station will be a huge benefit if it is used for the benefit of the islanders here. Just be alert," Foxy warns.

John promises Foxy that he will keep a faithful watch.

Meanwhile back in Puerto Padre...

Antonio Morales is conducting research in the area of bomb-making with various-size options and destructive capacity. He looks for new and inventive materials and containment options that may not be easily detected. The current devices are more readily identified by authorities. The use of dogs and chemical tests have made the explosives of the past too easily detectable. People like Antonio have to be more inventive and creative in crafting these devices now.

An opportunist and comrade in the Virgin Islands gives Antonio a call. "Comrade Morales, this is Manuel Garcia. I may have some news that will help you in your search for, shall I say, certain items of interest in your quest."

Manuel is currently located in the British Virgin Islands on Tortola and works in Soper's Hole Marina off of Frenchman's Cay. He is an anti-capitalist and is deeply rooted in his beliefs. His family dates back to the days of the island's slave trade. He has been told stories handed down from generation to generation about how the Europeans came to exploit the sugarcane and sugar-beet trade by taking over the land and using the local inhabitants to tend the field. The conditions were brutal and the tales vividly depressing. It took centuries to rid the islands of the Europeans but, eventually, the islands gained their independence one by one.

"What have you discovered that may be of interest to our cause?" Morales asks.

"There is a device that has been placed in a few locations on this island, as well as on a few other neighboring islands," Garcia responds. "I only know that it is a power-generating device. It is simple but radically effective. Based on my research, and after questioning some of the locals, this device apparently utilizes a fusion reaction as its source for generating power. Fusion, as you know, is the same process that powers the sun and creates huge amounts of energy, several times greater than fission. It also doesn't produce highly radioactive fission products. There is a lot of research and work going on in the field and, apparently, somebody has not only solved it, but they are also utilizing it with working devices."

"I am aware of the differences. I was unaware that somebody had been able to create a working device." Morales offers. "Do some more research into this. I will also get to work and research from this end and see what information we can dig up."

"We know that there are nuclear devices, including homemade bombs, out there but the problem is with procuring the uranium needed to activate them. What if we could find a way to reengineer the fusion device and create a weapon?" Garcia asks. "It would be much harder to detect, since it wouldn't produce the radioactive signal found in the fission-activated armaments of today."

"Find out exactly where and how many of these things are out there. Find out who controls them," Morales instructs.

"Will do, comrade," Garcia says.

Chapter 6

Virgin Power and Water is in the final planning stages for outfitting small to mid-size boats with the Ben Burns Power Station. Mass production is planned but won't be realized for a while. They are trying to prevent causing an imbalance in demand for traditional boat builds by flooding the market with their boats powered with the fusion generator. Alistair and Richard feel discretion is important and are continuing research and testing. Work also continues on developing the floating-home concept in conjunction with Alistair James' team of scientists.

Shawn calls up Alistair. He tells him that he would like to have the *Migration* outfitted with a Ben Burns Power Station. The *Migration* is a Manta 42. The vessel is designed with storage and a cockpit that can control every aspect of the ship when under sail.

The Manta's twenty-one-foot beam and narrow hulls spread beneath a pod. The width gives her stability against the lateral press of sails, and the narrow hulls allow the boat to slice, rather than plow, through the water. On deck, the boat has one winch—an electric, two-speed Harken—mounted on the cabin top just forward of the steering station. All reefing lines, halyards and sheets are led to this single point in the cockpit, so there's little need to go forward until the hook is dropped and the sails are furled. The Manta's simple rig includes a rigid, permanently adjusted boom and a modestly sized self-tending jib, which can be sheeted in by hand if necessary. The catamaran is a good vessel; a good cruising home as well as a reliable offshore boat.

He further explains to Alistair that, once outfitted, he is going to sail the *Migration* to Cayman Brac. "A friend and I are embarking on a treasure hunt and we could use living space at the site. In addition, we could certainly use some equipment and a trusted team of divers," Shawn continues.

"I will be happy to assist, Shawn," Alistair says. "In fact, I'm even willing to participate. I've done some diving in my day."

"Of course you have, Alistair!" Shawn responds enthusiastically.

Treasure hunting and salvage is not for the faint of heart or the financially strapped. It is an extensive, laborious, expensive and tedious task. In addition to the *Migration* to live aboard, they will need at least two additional boats for hauling equipment they will use to detect anomalies and targets on and under the sea floor. They will need two types of towfish to pull behind a powerboat. A towfish is a torpedo-shaped cylinder, manufactured as either a side-scan sonar or magnetometer. It is usually towed three ship lengths behind the boat to ensure that its vibrations and structure do not interfere with the data collection. The side-scan sonar sends a burst of acoustic energy out from both sides of the instrument. The acoustic energy bounces off any object that isn't buried and echoes back to the vessel. A transducer receives the echo and produces a computer-enhanced image of the object. Side-scan sonars offer detection as deep as one hundred and fifty feet and as wide as twenty-four feet.

A magnetometer is a passive survey instrument that does not send out any signals but picks up any object's signal within the earth's magnetic field. The magnetic disturbance will depend on the object's material, size and depth under the sediment. Iron objects will typically cause the most significant disturbance, but shallow and larger non-iron items could also cause a considerable change in the magnetic field.

A boat-towed magnetometer is the most powerful device for detecting iron and steel. These devices also use a towfish, and since they compare the intensity and direction of the magnetic field to one another, they seem to give more accurate readings.

With these devices, large areas of the seafloor are scanned, making them proficient and economical instruments. The magnetometer can pick up a shipwreck from up to one thousand feet away.

Because they will be working in water ranging from relatively shallow to moderate depth, they will need one or more Remote Operated Vehicles (ROVs). These are unmanned vehicles that are highly maneuverable and operated remotely by humans topside. ROVs typically tether to the operator or ship by a series of cables, making them slightly more limited in their ability than Autonomous Underwater Vehicle (AUVs). An ROV can send back video and other valuable information without risking human time and safety.

ROVs can utilize many different useful accessories. Hydraulics, cables, cameras and lighting equipment help to survey underwater landscapes and potential wrecks. Side sonars and magnetometers have proven more useful when used in conjunction with them. They can work to depths approaching fifteen thousand feet, depending on specifications. The ROV Shawn is acquiring will be working in depths much shallower.

Finally, they will need underwater metal detectors. These devices can withstand pressure at great depths and are useful after defining smaller target areas. When Shawn and Jackson pinpoint a search area, these units are perfect for defining individual targets. Underwater handheld metal detectors eliminate the effects of highly mineralized water and magnetic black sand, giving a signal only when a metallic object is present. They can be used to a depth of two hundred feet and have a search coil that is permanently attached to a control box. Headphones are also hardwired to the control box and have a robust volume control for hearing underwater.

Shawn tells Alistair, "I know we'll have the *Migration*, but we'll need a couple other vessels to tow the magnetometer and the side-scan radar units, and the other to deploy the ROV, as well as divers with metal detectors. If we can utilize both in coordination, we can cover a lot of seafloor and narrow our search grid considerably. Jackson and I will start working on obtaining the additional vessels and the search equipment. Then we'll fly back to Islamorada to get the *Migration* and sail her back here. It shouldn't take us much time at all."

"That sounds like a good plan. In the meantime, I'll dispatch Ethan and Aiden to Bud N' Mary's Marina and get them started on the conversion. They could use a mini-vacation anyway." Alistair chuckles. "Let's get busy then. We'll compare notes and set up some timeframes once you get the *Migration* on site near Cayman Brac."

"Okay, Alistair. That sounds great! I have lots of interesting thoughts and ideas to share with you. Jackson, my good friend and partner in crime, has just about got me convinced that there is treasure to be found at this location," Shawn says. "I am enthusiastically in!"

"In for a penny," Alistair says.

"In for a pound," Shawn replies. And they end their conversation.

Chapter 7

Ian and Hannah spend the better part of a month sailing in the Virgin Islands. Each stop entails spending time with the local caretaker of a Ben Burns Power Station. They make several uneventful stops to this point with only a few more islands to visit. Ian takes detailed notes about each unit, its location, its caretakers, any issues they may have, either with the unit or with people snooping about and asking questions about a power unit. Just like the original unit on Jost Van Dyke, all the units are still humming along without incident.

"I am so glad that my job now is to sail about the islands on this beautiful catamaran with absolutely breathtaking views," Ian says, lowering his Costa sunglasses and peering over the top of them at Hannah. She is oblivious to his inuendo, as she is busily checking the charts to make sure they are where they think they are. "Hey, I'm talking about you, Miss Flynn," Ian says, slightly annoyed.

"What? I'm busy reading the charts," Hannah replies.

"Never mind," Ian says. "The mood is ruined now. Where does your chart place the *Second Wind* at the moment?"

"Fifteen nautical miles south of Setting Point on Anegada," Hannah says with confidence.

Anegada is the northernmost of the British Virgin Islands. It lies approximately fifteen miles north of Virgin Gorda. Anegada is the only inhabited British Virgin Island formed from coral and limestone, rather than being of volcanic origin. While the other islands are mountainous, Anegada is flat and low. Its highest point is only about twenty-eight feet above sea level, earning the island its name, which is the Spanish term for the flooded land, "tierra anegada."

The primary business of Anegada is tourism. On a typical day during the tourist season, the island will have an additional two hundred to three hundred visitors. Commercial fishing is also a substantial business, with local fishermen providing most of the fresh fish and lobster catch for the rest of the British Virgin Islands.

Anegada has miles of white-sand beaches and the eighteen-mile-long Horseshoe Reef, one of the largest barrier coral reefs in the Caribbean.

"Horseshoe Reef is off limits so we'll sail and moor at Setting Point. We can take the dinghy in from there," Ian says. "We'll rent a Mini Moke and make our visit to The Settlement where the Ben Burns unit is housed sometime tomorrow, mid-morning."

The reef makes navigation to Anegada difficult. While charter boats freely sail among most of the other Virgin Islands, charter companies often forbid clients to sail to Anegada, to avoid running aground on the reef.

The reef has caused hundreds of shipwrecks, including HMS *Astraea* in 1808, the *Donna Paula* in 1819, and the MS *Rocus* in 1929. As such, it was once an important scuba-diving destination. In an effort to protect the reef, the British Virgin Islands government has made anchoring on Horseshoe Reef illegal.

Anegada is also known for the large salt ponds that cover much of the west end of the island. These ponds, which support unique fauna, were designated a Ramsar Site on May 11, 1999. In the 1830s, thousands of Caribbean flamingos lived in these ponds, but they were hunted for food and feathers throughout the nineteenth and early twentieth centuries and disappeared by 1950. They have since been re-established. As of 2016, the flamingo flock numbers approximately two hundred birds.

Anegada is a beautiful island, in part due to its unique geography. Ian and Hannah are on the bow of the *Second Wind*, now moored at Setting Point along with at least twenty other boats.

"Look at that sunset, Hannah!" Ian exclaims, almost spilling his Ketel One and coconut water as he points toward the horizon.

"I see them all the time now and I never get tired of the colors," says Hannah in awe. "Oranges, reds, yellows and purples that just have to be seen to be appreciated. Each seemingly unique in its own way. I love them! And I love you too!" She leans over and kisses him deeply. They stay on deck until the sun has set and the sky and sea grow dark.

The next morning, after a passionate night of love-making and a fitful night's sleep, they're back on deck enjoying their morning coffee and some guava pastries they had on hand from a previous stop on Virgin Gorda. "So, the plan today is take the dinghy to shore. We can walk to the island rental shack and rent a Mini Moke to get us around for the day," Ian says as he finishes his coffee.

The Mini Moke is a small, front-wheel-drive utility vehicle conceived and manufactured as a lightweight military vehicle by British Motor Corporation and subsequently marketed for civilian use under the Austin, Morris, Leyland and Moke brands. The name Moke combines Mini with Moke, which is an archaic term for a mule. The Moke is known for its simple, straightforward, doorless design, and for its adaptability. The Moke is the original and is slightly larger than the Mini. A typical Mini Moke is approximately ten feet in length and four feet in width. They are very popular modes of transport in the islands around the Caribbean.

"Sounds good to me, captain," Hannah says to Ian. "I'm going to shower and get dressed for the days adventure."

Ian replies, "I'll clear the plates and the cups and meet you back here in a few."

The Mini Moke is easy to maneuver on the sometimes narrow island roads, but they are a minimalist vehicle. Properly padded seats would be considered a luxury.

Ian and Hannah make their way to The Settlement where they meet with James Piper. James is one of the close confidants that Foxy Caldwell has recommended as guardian and caretaker of the Ben Burns Power Station. Anegada has only approximately three hundred residents, all living in The Settlement. The power station has been properly placed and housed, as with all the units they have seen on the other islands.

"It's working tirelessly and without any incidents at all. I mean, it has been running twenty-four hours a day, seven days a week since we installed it. We check the intake from the ocean every day to make sure it is clear of any debris or obstructions. That's about all the maintenance that's required. The Ben Burns Power Station is such a blessing to us on the island and we are most appreciative of having it in our hands," James says to Ian and Hannah.

"It's an amazing piece of equipment and I've seen the other units are working just as well as yours." Ian replies. "Obviously, you can contact Foxy anytime with any questions, but in the event he's not available, do you have the list of phone contacts who can assist you day or night?"

"Yes, I do. And I thank you for all the support and the confidence you have in me, and all of us on Anegada," James replies.

"Great then. Hannah and I will be on our way and leave you to your beautiful island. I hope you have great success in all you do until I see you again!" Ian says.

"Ian and I are going to take our Mini Moke around the island and see all the natural sites before setting sail again," Hannah says.

"Enjoy your time here and we'll look forward to seeing you soon!" James says, shaking hands with Ian and Hannah to bid them farewell.

Ian and Hannah complete their site-seeing adventure and return the Mini Moke to the rental shack before returning to the *Second Wind* for one more night at Setting Point. They are setting sail in the morning for Peter Island.

Chapter 8

Jean Pierre's brief flight from Port-o-Prince is quick and uneventful. Having only a small backpack as luggage, he makes his way through the front entrance of Hermanos Ameijeiras Airport. He exits into bright sunshine and extreme humidity. Things he is accustomed to in his homeland. A few minutes later, a man fitting the description he's been given approaches.

"Mr. Jean Pierre. My name is Antonio Morales. I am very glad to meet you. Please, if you will, my car is just over there in the parking area. I am looking forward to our discussions. Let's find a place where we can have lunch and get to know each other a little more." Antonio, who is slightly smaller than Jean at just under six feet tall, extends his hand to shake Jean Pierre's and looks up at his new acquaintance.

Jean says, "That will be an emphatic yes on both suggestions."

With that, the two get into Antonio's Beijing BJ212 hardtop. One of the most common 4x4s in Cuba, the SUV has been produced by Beijing Automotive Works since 1965. It uses a 2.4-liter, four-cylinder engine. The BJ212 is most closely related to early post-war Russian GAZ and UAZ 4x4s, even though its exterior tries to mimic everything from the Land Rover Series I to the Toyota Land Cruiser, with a little Jeep thrown in.

Antonio makes the drive down to the waterfront in Puerto Padre and parks outside a seaside establishment, the Restaurante & Cocteleria La Sicilia. "This place, believe it or not, has fine Italian food, as well as some of the best local fish in town. I hope that you will enjoy."

Not sure exactly what to order, Jean plays it safe with an order of the fresh catch, a grilled whole snapper served with vegetables. Antonio goes for the

Italian selection of spaghetti and meatballs. They get to know each other through some casual conversation over lunch, and then Antonio suggests they go back to his office in the warehouse, not too far from their current location, for more in-depth discussions about the opportunity they have in working together.

After a brief drive to the warehouse that serves as Antonio Morales' headquarters in Puerto Padre, he and Jean Pierre sit down in folding metal chairs at a modest worn wooden desk. They sit face-to-face. Antonio asks Jean to share with him his vision for the betterment of the Haitian people.

"I want to end the pilfering and redirection of the aid that comes to Haiti. The politicians simply siphon off the majority of aid and redirect it to their private bank accounts in the Caymans or in Switzerland. If even fifty percent of what is sent to us made it to the people, we would greatly increase our standard of living. We could raise ourselves out of the impoverished conditions we are forced to live in. Additionally, I want to reeducate the Haitian people to develop the land, rather than destroy it. Right now, they cut down trees to make charcoal for heat and with which to cook, and have no regard for what that does to the land. The top soil erodes. Storms produce mudslides because there is nothing to absorb the rainfall or the runoff. I want them to learn how to care for the land, how to be self-sufficient, how to prosper. But we must remove the corruption and that is the first and most difficult step. It's where I need monetary support. I also need able bodies to help with any insurrection."

Morales leans back in the chair and clasps his hands behind his head. He listens intently to Pierre's thoughts. He unclasps his hands and leans gently forward. "Those are worthy goals. I did not hear how you intend to remove the government officials and replace them. How are you planning to fund your rebellion? What kind of armed militia are you going to recruit?"

"That's my dilemma," Jean Pierre says flatly.

They continue to talk over the course of the next several hours. Antonio is gauging how far his new friend, Jean, is willing to go to achieve his goals.

"Are you willing to eradicate those stealing from your people? Are you willing to kill them?" Antonio interjects into the conversation.

Jean Pierre contemplates the question and pauses for several minutes. "I am not a violent person and I am not one who believes that killing solves the issues with which we are faced. I have concerns about taking another person's life."

Antonio elects not to press Jean on this point any further during this conversation. He'll propose it again at a later date.

As their conversation comes to an end, Antonio offers Jean a ride to the guest house he has arranged for his stay. Bonneville Place guest house at Flor Crombet 117, Puerto Padre 77200, Cuba. A modest house but very convenient for access to town and near Antonio's warehouse.

As they are preparing to leave, the phone rings. Antonio walks over and answers with, "Hello."

On the other end, Manuel Garcia says, "The unit in question is being moved within the week from St. Thomas to Acklins Island in the Bahamas."

"Excellent," Antonio replies. "I'll be on the way there in four days." He turns to Jean Pierre, puts a hand on his shoulder and says, "We may be on our way to providing a solution for your situation, my friend."

And, with that, they exit the warehouse.

Chapter 9

"Shawn, it's Ethan. Just wanted to let you know that Aiden and I have installed the unit you requested on the *Migration*. It's been tested and it's ready for you to pick up."

"Thank you so much, Ethan. Tell Aiden I appreciate your help with this. Hey, why don't you guys sail with me back to Cayman Brac and help us dig up some buried treasure?" Shawn asks.

"While that sounds inviting, we have to get back to work with Emma on the designs for the floating-homes, as well as a pipeline concept we've modeled on paper. We're attempting to expand the availability of the unit. So it's back to Miami and then off to sunny London," Ethan says, a little disappointed.

"I understand. Looking forward to not only seeing the results of your work but also experiencing the floating home. I just think it's such a fantastic and environmentally sound idea. Good luck, mate. You and Aiden have a safe trip back home, and say hi to Emma and George. And hello to the boss too." Shawn laughs as they say their goodbyes.

Shawn's plan is to fly to Miami and drive a one-way rental car back to Islamorda to pick up the *Migration*. He'll sail back to Cayman Brac and set up the boat as either primary or secondary living quarters. Then he and Jackson will have the other vessels brought on site to begin the actual search for the treasure.

After speaking with Alistair, they decide they will need a main boat as the main search vessel, one dive boat, and one boat to tow the magnetometers. Through their research, they decide they will locate and bring in a ship much like the *Magruder*, the ship Mel Fisher used to locate the *Nuestra Señora de Atocha*, the treasure found by Mel Fisher and his crew. The *Magruder* is eighty-one feet in length with nearly twenty-three-foot breadth, powered by twin Detroit diesel engines and twin thirty-kilowatt Kabota generators. She's outfitted with four- to twelve-inch airlifts, with a CP120 air compressor and a Bauer 20 cfm SCUBA air compressor. The ship also has twin prop deflectors called mailboxes, which were invented by Mel Fisher. Alistair, through his numerous connections, has found a similar ship in the Bahamas that has been used in a few treasure-hunting expeditions around the Bahama island chain. The *Marauder* is slightly smaller but outfitted similarly to the *Magruder*.

Alistair also locates two additional boats needed for diving and towing. He finds a thirty-foot Island Hopper flybridge dive boat, which will be used extensively in the initial underwater searches. The other boat is a Sea Hunt Gamefish 30 with center console for towing the magnetometers. It is ideally a fishing boat but it is available in Grand Cayman and will do the job they need. Once the *Migration* is in place off Cayman Brac, the other two locally procured vessels will be brought in. The *Marauder* will begin transit in a few days' time.

Shawn and Jackson agree that any search and excavation will be done in an eco-friendly manner. Great care will be given to not harming or destroying any reefs through mass excavation or use of explosives. These methods are used by other salvers and, while they are effective, they damage or destroy the seafloor, with no care to whatever else is in the water. The "mailboxes" or prop deflectors, assist in that effort and also help to clear the water and make visibility much better for the divers.

Next comes the crew. They'll need alternating teams of divers, two to a team. They need a captain for the *Marauder* and the pilots for the dive boat and the tow boat. They could get away with one captain to pilot both the other boats because they won't operate all three boats simultaneously. They will need another four crew members to do work topside and analyze data retrieved and examine any materials recovered. Seafarer Exploration, a treasure-seeking company operating in Florida is also a developer of exploration technology. They have created a sub-bottom sonar that allows searchers to actually see below the sea floor. Jackson has contracted for one to be shipped to Islamorda. They'll pick it up at Bud N' Mary's marina along with the *Migration*.

Shawn, Jackson, Alistair and George make four crewmen. They'll need a minimum of six more.

Alistair says he will contact his long-time confidant and best friend, David Smith, who he has worked with since they were young recruits in the British Armed Forces. David is in charge of several elite teams who eradicate evil from society, totally covert and without fanfare. He and his teams have had great success over the years. David Smith is a cover name for the Englishman, who has very deep connections through his time in the military and, subsequently, MI6. The name was selected as his alias because it consisted of the most common first and last name at the time in Britain.

"David will tell us who to add to our crew. I know that his recommendations will have the utmost discretion when it comes to our search."

"Sounds like a great idea, Alistair. I know having worked with Mr. Smith myself that he is the best person to provide us with a good team of individuals well versed in the art of search. And you know they'll be well-schooled in protection and self-defense," Shawn laughs.

Shawn Masters was one of David Smith's best recruits, but recently, Shawn retired from that line of work. He is smart, fast, effective and thorough. Mr. Smith wants his team members to have a life, or at least the cover of a life in normal society. It helps keep them fresh and sane. He has tried several times to lure Shawn out of retirement, but those efforts keep getting thwarted.

Alistair has military experience and, on more than one occasion, that experience has led him and David Smith to be in the same theater of operation. Their friendship is solid. Alistair's military duties, rank and discharge all remain a mystery to most. He served in a branch of the British Forces equivalent to that of the Navy Seals in the U.S. Armed Forces. To this day, he does not speak of his military career much and, even if he has the notion to discuss it, much of it remains classified.

The exploration for the Treasure of Lima cannot begin until the boats are on site. Jackson Collins decides he will accompany Shawn to retrieve the *Migration* and sail back with him from Islamorada. Once they cross the Florida Straits, the sail should be a boring ride across a beautiful sea containing every shade of blue. Jackson plans to spend his days studying tidal charts and researching major hurricanes that have passed over or near the site where they will be starting the search.

Jackson tells Shawn, "Treasure hunting is exciting and tedious. It took Mel Fisher over sixteen years from beginning the search to finding the motherlode. And, they continue to find artifacts to this day. We may not find anything. But, then again, we could get lucky."

"Well, luck be a lady tonight! Let's go and see what we can find!" Shawn replies.

Chapter 10

"Foxy, this is John from Acklins. I was ambushed shortly after you returned to Jost Van Dyke."

Foxy says, "Are you okay? What happened?"

John goes on to explain that the unit was working well and producing more than enough electricity to power Lovely Bay Settlement, along with an ample water supply. "Last night, I went to check on the unit and I was hit over the head and knocked out cold. I didn't see who did it or how many. When I came to a while later, the unit was gone—definitely stolen. They didn't know how to disconnect it properly so they ripped it lose. Bottom line, the unit is gone and I have no idea where it is."

"Are you going to be okay?" Foxy asks. "I'll alert the maker of the unit and see what, if anything, can be done."

"I'll be fine. Just a knot on my head. No concussion. Only a bad headache for a few days," John replies.

"Good. I'm glad you are going to fully recover. I'll be in touch soon," Foxy says.

As Foxy and John end their conversation, a Cigarette 38 Top Gun piloted by Antonio Morales with Jean Pierre on board is speeding back to Puerto Padre. The unit under a tarp in the cabin is secured with straps. The Cigarette 38 has a top speed of eighty-four miles per hour. Antonio has settled in at a more comfortable forty-six miles per hour, or forty knots, over relatively flat seas. They should make the trip from Lovely Bay Settlement to Puerto Padre in just under four hours.

The plan is get the unit straight to the warehouse and store it there for the time being. Even with the calm, clear conditions under the cloudless sky, there is not much conversation due to the noise of the engines and the wind whipping across the boat.

They cruise across the water silently as they return to Puerto Padre.

Jean Pierre contemplates the brief attack on Acklins. Once Antonio hit the islander on the head, he wanted to finish him off. Jean Pierre intervened and stopped Antonio from killing the innocent man. He is simply not a violent person and values human life a lot more than his current boat mate. He files the incident in the back of his mind and decides that, rather than confront Antonio Morales with his concern, he will be more cautious in his dealings with this supposed benefactor.

On the way to Jost Van Dyke...

"Alistair! It's Foxy!" he says into his satellite phone. "The unit we established on Acklins has been stolen. My friend and the caretaker there, John, were ambushed while checking on the unit last night," Foxy excitedly explains.

"Oh no, Foxy. That's terrible. Is your friend going to be okay? No long-term injuries suspected?" Alistair asks.

"Nothing long term. He's going to be just fine. How are we going to find the unit?" Foxy inquires.

"That isn't a problem." Alistair explains that the early units produced on Cave Cay did not have a tracking device. "However, after the situation with our friends in the Florida Keys and then Weston Stone trying to steal the unit, we created and began installing small, hidden, sophisticated GPS tracking devices in all units, whether they were stand-alone, installed on boats or used in the floating platforms. The one sent to Acklins did have a GPS locator. That unit is the last of the original devices that was stored in St. Thomas at the storage facility. I sent Emma, Ethan and Aiden to the facility to install the tracking devices on the nine units we stowed there." Alistair continues, "I wouldn't worry too much about the unit. Only a handful of people are capable of determining how it operates. And I know all of them. It is more important, I think, to see if we can determine who took it and what their endgame might be. In the meantime, please contact the caretakers of the other units we've deployed and put them on high alert. Be vigilant. Let's keep an eye on them twenty-four hours a day until we can figure this out."

"I'm ahead of you on that one. As soon as I heard from John, I immediately put our unit on Jost on high security alert and contacted all the other caretakers to do the same," Foxy stated.

"Excellent. We'll touch base soon. Stay safe," Alistair replied as he ended the call.

Chapter 11

Ian sits contently in the cockpit of the *Second Wind* and looks out over the bow, admiring the colors of the Caribbean. He leans over and kisses Hannah, who is sitting next to him, on the cheek.

"You missed," she says playfully as she turns and kisses him back on the lips. "There, that's better."

"I never get tired of this view and sailing these waters and seeing every shade of blue ever created. And then, of course, doing this with you!" Ian smiles as he looks at his shipmate in her emerald-green bikini and tan sun hat.

"I agree," she says as she counts the number of blue colors she sees. "Royal blue, azure, sky blue, sapphire and crystal. I know the last one isn't technically blue but it is a fantastic, clear absence of color almost against the blue sky."

"I don't think I'm going to be a stickler on your color description, sweetheart," Ian replies as he settles back and sails on to Peter Island.

There is a small marina surrounded by Peter Island Resort. Sprat Bay is located on Peter Island, south of Tortola in the British Virgin Islands. Located five miles south of Fat Hogs Bay on Tortola and ten miles east of St. John., Ian has opted for a short stopover here to check the *Second Wind* for any maintenance needs after their island-hopping journey to check the Ben Burns Power Stations.

"Hannah, I'm going to run some checks. How about calling Sandra and letting her know we are on island and will be at the resort for a couple of days? Then we'll sail over to Thirty Steps Inn and catch up with her."

After nearly an hour, Hannah reboards their boat and tells Ian that Sandra had to seaplane over to St. Thomas to get a few supplies and maintenance items she could not obtain anywhere locally. "She'll be back the day after tomorrow," Hannah tells Ian.

"That will be perfect timing," Ian says. "I'm looking forward to seeing Sandra and what she's done with the Thirty Steps Inn."

The Thirty Steps Inn is a small, four-bedroom inn with a quaint bar made of coral and old ships' timbers, with seats made from cargo barrels and samplings of the finest rums on the islands. There is also an eight-table restaurant, or really, eating area, that serves a breakfast of local pastries and fruits, a lunch of pre-made sandwiches and made-to-order conch fritters and lobster rolls. Dinner is served only on the weekends and it consists of two or three of the chef's specials. Hannibal, the chef, serves local fish, lobster and, when available, beef from Tortola.

The inn dates back to the 1800s and is suspected of once being the home of one of the area's notorious pirates, but no evidence has been found to substantiate that claim. It has been repurposed as a small island inn, an alternative to the more bustling Peter Island Resort. The name, Thirty Steps Inn, comes from the thirty rock and coral steps that lead to the inn's front door from the two boat slips at the small wooden dock below. Because they are made of coral, they still shimmer a pinkish color when the sun hits them in the afternoon.

Ian completes the minor repairs and maintenance checks on the *Second Wind*. Hannah restocks the supplies and assists Ian with the maintenance and repairs. Ian is teaching Hannah all about the *Second Wind*. He wants Hannah to know every nuance of the boat, including sailing her in and around the Virgin Islands, and eventually, beyond.

Hannah is a quick learner and soon masters the tasks she's given. "You're doing a spectacular job!" Ian tells her as he repairs one of the sail riggings.

"Thank you, Captain. I have a really wonderful instructor guiding me along," Hannah laughs as she replies.

"I'll make us dinner tonight. Some savory pasta with vodka sauce, Caesar salad and cheesy garlic bread," Ian says, awaiting her approval.

"And a nice Pinot Noir to compliment that menu!" Hannah says. "But first, I'm going to try to get some sun time in on the bow. Let me know when you're ready to begin meal preparation, sir." She winks at him as she makes her way forward to catch the rays from the high, white sun above Sprat Bay.

Ian takes the time to phone Shawn and finally get caught up on each other's activities over the past couple of months. "Shawn, it's Ian. How goes the treasure hunting?"

"Ian! Great to hear from you. As you know, there's a great deal of preparation before we even think about diving. In fact, I spoke to Alistair, who's assisting us in getting the proper boats to the site off Cayman Brac. I'm currently bringing the *Migration*, which was still docked in Islamorada since our first adventure with the James crew. Ethan and Aiden outfitted it with a Ben Burns Power Station. I'm currently south of the western tip of Cuba, making way for Cayman Brac," Shawn explains. "Jackson is with me and we picked up a sub-bottom sonar that allows us to see below the seafloor. It'll save us a ton of bottom time."

"That's fantastic!" Ian says. "Hannah and I have been sailing around the islands checking on the Ben Burns Power Stations that Alistair has deployed with Foxy's assistance. We're on Peter

Island now and are heading to see Sandra in just a few hours."

"Sounds great. I talk to her each day. I think she might be growing a bit tired of the innkeeper life. I told her she can come here and help find buried treasure anytime she wants. Same holds for you and Hannah."

"I'll certainly keep that in mind. Although, if you recall when we end up together, this strange thing happens. People shoot at us." Ian laughs out loud. "Maybe this time, we can break that trend. After our stop with Sandra, we're going to sail over to Jost Van Dyke to see Foxy. I need to review my observations and data with him regarding the power stations. You have safe travels and we'll catch up soon," Ian says as they end their conversation.

Later, at Sandra's...

"I think I've had my fun running the inn. I have the desire to get back out there and travel some.

I love the inn but I can't run it and travel. Plus, I miss Shawn and, even though I talk to him nearly every day, it's not the same. You get that, don't you, Hannah?" Sandra asks.

"I do," Hannah replies, thinking back to a prior life where she was separated from and then lost her lover. "Have you thought about hiring someone to manage the place while you're gone?

"I have. I've even had some interviews. But I would still be responsible for the inn, so I'd worry about it and would need to come back often. No, I think if I am going to leave here, then I'm going to sell it. But to who and for how much?" Sandra ponders her own question.

Ian says, "Sandra, you know Zach from back home? Zach's Place by the ocean? Let me get in touch with him. He's a smart entrepreneur who might want to expand his holdings. He has three bar and restaurant locations back home. Maybe he's ready to be a caretaker of an inn in a

Caribbean paradise. Keep the names of the people you interviewed to manage the place. I don't know if he would be full-time here because of his other interests. Plus, he and his wife, Emalee, just had their first child."

"I would love to sell it to someone I know. That would be ideal," Sandra replies.

"Okay, I'll get in touch with him and gauge his interest." With that, Ian goes out on the veranda overlooking the Caribbean with Tortola in the distance.

Chapter 12

Antonio Morales stares at the device sitting on the table in his warehouse in Puerto Padre, a very puzzled look on his face. He hasn't tried to dismantle the unit yet. The device is slightly larger than a commercial microwave oven. He holds his chin in his right hand as he ponders and says to himself, "How does this produce enough heat to even create the fusion reaction? It's so small." He decides that he needs to consult a colleague in Havana who has much more experience in nuclear devices than himself.

"Department of Energy," the uninspired female voice answers in a thick Latin accent. "How may I direct your call?" she continues in her robotic tone.

"Hello, this is Antonio Morales. May I speak to Renaldo Espinoza?"

"One moment, please."

Antonio listens to silence for approximately two minutes. Then, "Senor Morales. How have you been and how can I be of service to you."

"I have a situation that I need your assistance in analyzing," Antonio responds.

"Are you in your office in Havana?" Renaldo asks.

"No, I'm in a temporary location in Puerto Padre. Can you get here within a day or two?"

"Why do you require immediate attention. I have some pressing issues here that require my expertise."

Antonio says directly, "Comrade, I cannot discuss this over any open lines of communication. It's too delicate. I need you here. Come Friday afternoon and spend a day, or even two. I may have something that could have some very interesting possibilities for you and I."

Renaldo responds, "You've piqued my interest. Pick me up at the airport in Puerto Padre on

Friday. I'll email you my itinerary." And with that, Espinoza hangs up.

Jean Pierre listens to one side of the conversation. He asks, "So what now? We don't seem to have a great deal to go on. This... this thing! What the hell is it? What are we going to do with it? Are you going to ransom it? What could it be worth?"

"Stop with the questions!" Morales demands. I'll explain it to you when my friend and comrade Renaldo Espinoza gets here."

Renaldo Espinoza is a well-educated, middle-aged, fit communist party member, born to parents who hailed the Castro regime. He gained favor with the communist government as he progressed through school and his service in the military. He only served a short while before he began his government-sponsored career in energy and the development of alternate sources of power given Cuba's limited resources. Renaldo remains single but does not lack female companionship. Forty-five and physically striking with jet-black hair, clean-shaven and an islander's complexion. He cuts a handsome figure at government galas and celebrations. He enters Morales' warehouse.

"So, show me this device that you have captured but have no earthly idea how it works," Renaldo half-snapped at Antonio.

"I can only tell you what I know," Antonio says. He then begins to recount the information on the device that he has ascertained from his cohort on Tortola, Manuel Garcia. He explains how he came to capture the device on Acklins a short time ago. "I know that it uses nuclear fusion to create power and provides clean drinking water as a by-product."

"What is it that you intend to do with this device, Antonio?" Renaldo says as he glances at Jean Pierre.

"I'm trying to assist my friend Jean with his dream to start and succeed with a revolution in his home country, Haiti. To root out and replace the corrupt government politicians and decision-makers with those who want to improve his native land. As a bonus to us in Cuba, he will be loyal to our cause and help us with operations and movement of goods and services that further our influence in the region," Antonio replies before continuing, "Any successful revolt requires money, weapons and a loyal army of followers. So the first step is money. My thought is to repurpose the fusion device into a bomb that we would use to ransom a great deal of cash. That will get us started."

"Interesting concept. Let me take and examine this device. I'll see what I can ascertain about it, its components and its best use to us and, of course, to Mr. Pierre's revolution," Renaldo states flatly.

"As a side note, if this device really works as you say producing power and potable water, why don't you figure out how to operate it. If our Cuban leaders can't figure it out, maybe our friends in Russia or China would be interested in it—for the right fee, of course" Renaldo finishes his thought.

"I have already contacted several of our government leaders and they have no interest in the device. Not surprising, to be honest. I also made contact, both directly and by third party, to the sources we have in the foreign governments. Nobody seems to be interested in this particular device. They say they have people working day and night on ways to utilize fusion to create power and provide valuable by-products. I implored them to at least take a look but they brushed me off, so here we are."

Jean Pierre remains quiet. He reflects on the conversation. He thinks to himself, "What if we tried to replicate the device? What if we could provide unlimited power and clean drinking water to the people? Why do we have to make a bomb?'' He is alone with his thoughts.

Renaldo and Antonio start to examine the device.

Chapter 13

As far as physical size, Cayman Brac lies in between Grand Cayman and Little Cayman. Cayman Brac is fourteen miles long and just over one mile wide. It has impressive limestone cliffs running along the middle of the island from west to east. At the eastern tip, the bluff ends in a dramatic one-hundred-and-forty-foot drop.

The island derived its name from these cliffs, since "brac" is the Gaelic word for bluff. The island has become a destination for experienced rock climbers who want to take on the challenge of climbing these cliffs.

Cayman Brac has the highest elevation in the Cayman Islands of one hundred and fifty-two feet. The island is dotted with many caves, which are carved out of the rock formations. Island legend has it that pirates hid treasures in these caves, although no pirates' treasure has ever been found. Amateur and professional treasure seekers exploring the caves have found random coins but not much more. There are hazards in the caves, including watching the tides, taking care not to not get stuck at high tide. Also, the caves are a haven for bats, and there is even a Bat Cave on the island.

Cayman Brac, as a tourist destination, is much more low-key than Grand Cayman. There are no high-rise hotels, gourmet restaurants or glitzy shopping malls. That's where staying on Grand Cayman would be a better bet. Much of the Cayman Brac shoreline is rocky and coral-strewn. The island's population is in the neighborhood of two thousand full-time residents.

Shawn has sailed the *Migration* to the initial search point agreed upon by he and Jackson. Jackson himself has arranged the Island Hopper dive boat and Sea Hunt Gamefish 30. He has these currently anchored off the southern coast of Cayman Brac. This is where the initial search commences. Alistair is with George and they are sailing the *Marauder* from Bimini to Cayman Brac under the captaincy of Richard Jones, an experienced seafarer provided by David Smith. Accompanying them will be Paul Arkin, an expert underwater welder with vast diving experience. Also, Scotty Emmons, a veteran Navy diver with a lengthy resume of overt, as well as covert, diving adventures.

There are a couple of related, prominent geographic challenges to treasure hunting in the Caymans: the Cayman Trench and the Cayman Ridge. Jackson explains to Shawn, "The Cayman Trench is a submarine trench on the floor of the western Caribbean Sea between Jamaica and the southeastern tip of Cuba. The trench is also known as the Cayman Trough, Bartlett Deep, or Bartlett Trough. It is the deepest point in the Caribbean Sea and plummets to a maximum depth of twenty-five thousand, two hundred and seventeen feet."

"That's nearly five miles to the bottom!" Shawn exclaims. "There's no way we could even remotely explore that depth."

"You are absolutely correct! If our shipwreck slid down the ridge, she is going to be there for a very long time."

Jackson continues, "Adjacent to the Cayman Trench lies the Cayman Ridge, an undersea mountain range tracing the northern margin of the trench in the Caribbean Sea, including the Cayman Islands. It extends approximately nine hundred and thirty miles from the Sierra Maestra in southern Cuba to the Misteriosa Bank. The part of the ridge that protrudes through the sea creates Grand Cayman, Little Cayman and Cayman Brac."

Shawn chimes in, So, our focus will need to be on the more shallow waters just off the southern shores of Cayman Brac. I suppose you will want to explore the southern coast and then we'll work our way west to east up to the bluff. If we haven't found anything of consequence, we then continue back east to west along the northern coast."

Jackson responds, "That's the plan. And if we find nothing at all, we're out a bunch of money and time."

Chapter 14

Ian calls Alistair to report on the units and their status, which he and Hannah have checked on during their recent tour.

"What do you mean, one is missing?" Ian half yells into the satellite phone.

"The last of the original units we produced on Cave Cay in the Exumas was personally delivered by Foxy to one of his friends on Acklins Island in the southern Bahamas. It was stolen. Had we not taken steps after the previous attempts to illegally obtain or destroy the units, we would have no idea where to look. At this moment in time, the Acklins unit is sitting in a warehouse district in Puerto Padre, Cuba," Alistair explains. "Many months ago, we decided it would be prudent to halt production until Emma could get the tracking system operational. Now that it is, we're producing units with the GPS tracking chip and we'll know where each and every unit is at any given time. There are also a handful of units we have produced through Virgin Power and Water that contain the GPS tracker. I'm having Emma create the tracking chip for the units we initially produced and deployed in the Virgin Islands, including Foxy's. I'll have Emma ship them out to Tortola. If you and Hannah would be so kind as to revisit those units and install the chip, I would be greatly appreciative. For now, we will continue to monitor the unit that is in Cuba."

"You know that I would be more than happy to assist you in any way," Ian says, and then blurts out, "Cuba? Why do you think the unit is sitting in Cuba? Do you think the Cuban government would give their people access to free water and power?"

"No, I really don't think so. If they know it's a fusion reactor, they may be trying to get the technology to the Chinese or the Russians. I would be happy if they were going to use the device for the good of their people. However, I have to assume they may be trying to determine if the Ben Burns Power Station could be repurposed into a nuclear device, for military use or other purposes. I just don't know at this point."

"Could they make a bomb or some other weapon out of it, Alistair?" Ian asks anxiously.

"I suppose that an evil enough mind with the right technology and a dark enough agenda to destroy could possibly come up with something. But we took so many precautions with its development that I feel almost certain it cannot be repurposed. When the unit is dismantled, the fusion reactor will self-destruct and become useless if it is improperly handled. "

"That makes me feel a whole lot better, Alistair," Ian says. He then concludes his detailed verbal report on all the units he and Hannah inspected. "I'm quite confident that those units are secure and well-guarded. Have Emma get us the trackers, along with the instructions to install. Hannah and I will properly place them on the existing units that don't have them."

"That's good news, at least. And thank you for continuing to support and assist me in the development and monitoring of the power stations. I can't thank you enough," Alistair responds.

"You know we'll do whatever you ask. Where are you now?"

"Actually, I'm nearing Cayman Brac on the search vessel *Marauder* on our way to assist Shawn and his friend, Jackson, on their treasure hunt," Alistair says with a laugh.

"Did he con you into helping him in this adventure?"

"Not at all, Ian," Alistair replies. "I've done some diving in my day and George, who also has some experience, is with me. I'm looking forward to getting back in the water and scouring about. David Smith has gotten us an excellent captain and a couple of veteran divers. So, even if we don't find anything down there on the sea floor, it will be a very interesting vacation to say the least. If you and Hannah aren't busy once you've completed your inspections, you should join us."

"As a matter of fact, we're on Peter Island with Sandra, who has made an inquiry to a mutual friend to gauge his interest in purchasing her inn. If that goes well, and there are no other pressing matters, you might get all three of us to join you." Ian laughs. "I'll contact Shawn and discuss with him what they're going to do and how they plan to search the grid around Cayman Brac. But, as I always caution, when we all get together, people tend to try and shoot at us, so we need to think that through." He laughs again. "But we're certainly due a relaxing, non-violent adventure, free from evil-doers."

Alistair laughs this time. "I have to agree with that sentiment. Let me know what you decide. Who knows, we might actually find something down there." With well wishes, they end their call.

An hour later, Ian calls Shawn on the satellite phone to discuss the plans for the treasure search. Shawn explains at great length where they are searching and for what they are searching. After some back and forth, Shawn tells Ian that Jackson has documentation and solid leads that point to this location.

"I can't tell you more than that, even over the satellite phone, but he has convinced me that it could very well be here, or near here," Shawn says. "I'll let him explain everything to you in person if you decide to join us."

"I understand. You never know who might be listening to our conversations. Lots of bad people out there," Ian replies.

"We've attracted our fair share over the years. Jackson has flown back to Seville to review some of the research a friend of his has been doing at the

General Archives of the Indies' in Seville. I'm flying back to the NOAA offices in Miami to review the tide, temperature and weather mapping for the last couple of hundred years," Shawn concludes.

Chapter 15

Greg and Rachel from Springfield, Missouri are enjoying the Caymans as they celebrate twenty-five years of wedded bliss. One of the reasons they have had a successful union is through compromise and the ability to accommodate each other's interests.

They spend the first part of their anniversary on Grand Cayman. Rachel loves the food and wines and the shopping when they are on vacation. She likes to lie on the beach and by the pool to relax, absorbing as many of the sun's rays as possible while maintaining a mandatory buzz from the freshly made daiquiris and countless umbrella drinks.

Greg is more of a beach adventurer of sorts. He likes to snorkel and scuba dive. He also likes to walk the beach with his trusty metal detector and find lost trinkets. Greg will accommodate Rachel's indulgence into Grand Cayman and Rachel will, in turn, allow

Greg to ply his beachcomber skills later in their stay on Cayman Brac.

On the first part of the journey, they are splurging. Rachel wants luxury so Greg books them in at the Ritz-Carlton, Grand Cayman, located on spectacular Seven Mile Beach. White-sand beaches within steps of their suite. Water so clear that you cannot tell the difference between the pool and ocean. A spa and other amenities to make sure Rachel has a spectacular time. Greg has to admit that he does enjoy being pampered as well, he just does not admit it to Rachel.

On Cayman Brac, the choices are much less posh. They tend to be geared to the scuba diver. The resort Greg chooses is Cayman Brac Beach Resort, located on the western tip of the island at 383 Channel Road. It is a cozy but very nice forty-room resort. Greg is looking forward to some snorkeling, light diving and scouring the beach for treasure. Not much has been recovered from the many ships that have gone down in these waters. But the occasional coin or silver chain have been discovered from time to time.

Relieved to have concluded the first part of the anniversary in the bustling Grand Cayman, Greg now has four beautifully mundane days to snorkel, scuba dive some of the shallow reefs, and walk along the beach scanning with his trusty metal detector for any piece of treasure that may lay about. As metal detectors go, his is a Bounty Hunter TK4 Tracker IV, a popular detector. He chose it for traveling due to it being lightweight and easy to use. Two nine-volt batteries for power and off he can go. It will detect objects from six to ten inches below the sand, which is plenty for recovering coins, watches, chains and rings.

Rachel accompanies him on one snorkel trip but spends most of her day by the pool reading an assortment of books and listening to some music she downloaded to her cell phone. At the moment, she is sipping a frozen daiquiri made with Seven Fathoms Premium Rum and fresh guava, papaya and mango. The song that plays as she takes a nice, long sip is "Blame It on the Rum," a Sunny Jim White tune written when he was performing on Grand Cayman. The song was actually used in the movie *The Firm*. She closes her eyes and hums along with the music.

Greg decides to spend his last day combing the beach for trinkets. He patrols the beach along the resort on the southwestern side of Cayman Brac. He's found some American quarters, Canadian nickels and an English pound coin. Also a few bottle caps, a discarded piece of foil and a rusty nail of no historical significance. He turns and adjusts his path back toward the hotel area, where Rachel is on her third Seven Fathoms daiquiri and is now singing along with the late Jim Morris about "The Floating Opera."

Greg takes a hundred or so steps and his metal detector gets a hit. He digs down almost a foot into the white sand with his small trowel until he turns up a shiny, gold object. He raises his Oakley sunglasses to inspect what looks to be a coin, but is significantly worn. He tosses it in his small bag of "keepers"—those items that he decides may have some value that he'll check out when he returns home.

Chapter 16

The *Marauder* anchors off the south side of Cayman Brac, along with the Island Hopper and the Sea Hunt Gamefish 30. The *Migration* is also anchored near the *Marauder*.

Alistair spends some time sixty days prior to his arrival on site meeting virtually with officials in Grand Cayman concerning the treasure-hunting operation. The Cayman's take great pride in protecting and maintaining an ecological balance in their waters. Getting permits to conduct any sort of dredging is not normally allowed. Alistair assures them that the dredging will be minimal and done with minimal ecological impact. He explains the four watercraft they will be employing in their search, along with the technology they will be using. They will be deploying a sub-bottom sonar, allowing searchers to actually see below the sea floor without disturbing it. If they do find something, the sonar pinpoints the item and allows for precise excavation of the seafloor, rather than taking a wide swath of the area. Alistair explains to the government officials that protecting their reef is just as important to him and his search group as it is to the people of the Caymans. In addition to convincing the Cayman authorities to grant him the permits, he also has to negotiate with the Cayman government on how much they will want in royalties based on any finds Alistair and crew uncover in their search. Toward the end of the sixty-day effort, Alistair is granted his permits, along with strict rules for his operation, including the several areas which will be off limits. They also agree on a "fee" structure concerning any treasure found.

As they begin, there is a full crew, all with significant boating experience as well as underwater training. On site for the beginning of the search are Alistair, George, Shawn, Jackson, Scotty Emmons, Paul Arkin and Richard Jones. Jackson and Shawn commence the search with the tedious task of running a pattern with the towfish magnetometer, which resembles mowing a lawn but on a much grander scale. The objects they'll be searching for will almost certainly be under the sea floor. After a couple of hundred years of tides and currents, storms and shifting sands, anything of value or indicating a wooden vessel is not going to be sitting on the ocean floor. Wooden ships are preserved for a great deal of time in the seawater. The structural integrity of a vessel certainly would be hard to maintain after the currents and storms over the past couple of hundred years. Finding anything resembling a hull or mast of stern castle will have been compromised. The side-scan sonar towfish is available but likely will not be used anytime soon, if at all, because it's purpose is to identify objects and structures above the sea floor.

"As Shawn and I discussed early on, we'll start on the southern coast where the remnants of the old reef are and move through our grid pattern from west to east. As we round the bluffs on the far eastern side, we'll work our way back east to west," Jackson says to the entire group assembled on the deck of the *Marauder*.

"Because the *Migration* is outfitted with a Ben Burns Power Station, we can run the electrical needs through her. She'll also provide us with clean water for consumption, as well as the other ship's needs," Shawn adds.

The operation commences with anticipation but also the understanding that time and patience are their greatest assets for now.

Chapter 17

A month goes by and Alistair has Emma ship the tracking devices to the Terrance B. Lettsome International Airport on Beef Island, Tortola, BVI. Ian and Hannah sail there to pick up the GPS units and deliver them to the caretakers of the first Ben Burns Power Stations in operation.

Sandra opts to stay behind at the Thirty Steps Inn. She awaits the arrival of Zach and Emalee, who may be interested in purchasing the property on Peter Island.

With precise instructions from Emma James, who developed the GPS unit, Ian and Hannah retrace their voyage from a few months back to each unit's location. After a week and a half, they make their way back to Peter Island to check on Sandra and the status of the potential sale.

"Well, hello, Zach!" Ian shouts as he and Hannah enter the small outdoor patio with a beautiful view of Great Harbour. "How are you doing?"

"Great, Ian! So good to see you. Missed seeing you at Zach's Place. But if this is where you've been spending your time, then I understand why your presence has been scarce. I'd like you to meet my wife, Emalee. I don't think you two have met."

"Nice to meet you, Emalee. And this is Hannah."

Introductions, handshakes and hugs all around. They all take a seat at the table and visually breathe in the view of the clear blue sea. Sandra says, "I've been showing Zach around the area. I'm hoping maybe you could take us on a sail around the nearby islands to give him and Emalee a feel for the area, the commerce and the recreational activities."

"Absolutely! I'll be happy to. I will tell you that, if you do plan to buy the place, the preferred method of traveling around is by boat," Ian says with a smile. "Not the worst way to get around. Tomorrow morning, meet us just over there at Sprat Bay dock and we'll motor out to the *Second Wind*," Ian says as he points slightly to the east.

The next day, the group makes an early start and boards the *Second Wind* with the yellow sun just up over the horizon. Ian takes the group on a leisurely sail to some of his favorite spots in the area. They sail west into the sapphire waters of Pillsbury Sound between St. Thomas and St. John. They motor into Cruz Bay and find a mooring ball. While they ride the dinghy into town, Ian gives a short description of the area. "Cruz Bay is located on the west coast of St. John. It's the main hub of commerce and the commercial center of the island. This is the primary access point to the rest of island. Frequent barge and ferry services connect St. John to St. Thomas. Ferries also run regularly between Cruz Bay and Tortola, Virgin Gorda, and Jost Van Dyke in the British Virgin Islands. Make sure you take your passport when going to the BVI."

Ian continues, "There's plenty to do on the island and over two-thirds of the mountains, beaches and surrounding water are protected within the National Park Service. Great food, drink, snorkeling and hiking. Much more relaxed and less commercialized than St. Thomas. I love spending time here. In fact, the *Second Wind* is normally docked here when we're sailing about to other places. The Virgin Islands National Park Visitor Center, the Elaine Sprauve Library and a United States Post Office are also located in Cruz Bay."

"This is great! I understand why people want to live here year round. Where to next?" Zach asks.

"On to see a very dear friend and one of the most unique bars in the islands. On to Jost Van Dyke!" Ian exclaims.

An easy sail from Cruz Bay to Great Harbour on Jost. The winds are low and the water brilliant shades of blue and relatively calm. They tie up at the dock in Great Harbour. A short stroll down the crushed shell and coral road ending at Foxy's Tamarind Bar. Foxy isn't in today but Ian leaves word with his trusted manager that they stopped by.

"Let me get you a sampling of the tastes of our island," the manager says as he slaps Ian on the back. And, of course, some of Foxy's Punch!" Foxy's Punch is made with white rum, dark rum, cranberry, guava and lime.

They enjoy the punch as they are served jerk chicken wings, chicken roti and, of course, conch fritters. All Caribbean favorites. Ian gives them the history of Foxy and the bar. "Rather fascinating man and he does so much for the community and education. He has a rather impressive school set up for the children of the island."

Ian excuses himself to take a look at the ramshackle shed that houses the very first Ben Burns Power Station. It's still in good order and going strong. Returning to the group, he announces, "Now that we've had some good food and a couple of beverages, let's make the short trip to White Bay and a truly unique experience."

Zach and Emalee ask questions about the area and the locals and the tourism. Zach is a very bright and astute businessman, especially when it comes to the bar and restaurant business. This would be his first venture into a hotel-type operation. Most of his questions about that topic he directs to Sandra. "You've owned the inn for a few years now. Knowing what you know now, would you do it again? Any of the ins and outs of the operation that you would do differently? Do you have regular guests that come each year? How do you attract new guests?" Zach peppers Sandra with questions.

Sandra admits, like with any new venture, that she did not foresee some of the issues she had to endure. "Mostly maintenance issues. The inn has been around quite a while and it takes some work to keep up." She answers most of his other questions as Ian drops anchor in White Bay some thirty yards to shore.

"Okay, here we are," Ian announces.

"Do we take the dinghy?" Zach asks.

"Hell, no!" Ian laughs. "We're going to the Soggy Dollar Bar and Ivan's Honor Bar. The reason they called it the Soggy Dollar is that we have to swim to it. And your money is going to be wet so you pay with... soggy dollars... ta da!"

Ian and Hannah secure the anchor and they all eagerly jump in the crystal clear water and swim the short distance to the sugar white beach of White Bay. After a few pain killers and a walk over the rocky hill to Ivan's, Zach marvels at the place. "Wait, so there's no bartender, no waitresses, no manager?" Zach asks incredulously.

"No. It's an honor bar. You decide what you want to drink, write it down and put your money in the till. On your honor, so to speak. I don't see something like this making it anywhere else. For some reason, Ivan keeps the place humming along and people keep paying without being told to. Pretty amazing really."

They return to the *Second Wind* and, as everyone is getting settled, Ian's satellite phone rings. It's Foxy. "Ian, I just got back and find that I missed you and your friend. Where are you?"

"Just about to sail out of White Bay and back to Peter Island," Ian replies. "Are you at the Tamarind Bar right now."

"Sitting at my usual spot. If you have the time, sail back over and we'll spend some time."

After a quick show of hands, the group decides to return to Great Harbour and visit with the unofficial mayor of Jost Van Dyke. Foxy's Tamarind Bay on Great Harbour, just around the corner from where they are.

"I thought it would be very beneficial for you to talk to Foxy. I have a small bit of business to tend to with him. Then you can ask him any and everything about owning a bar and restaurant on the islands. And he can also tell you of the pitfalls of being an outsider, so to speak, and of owning a small establishment."

"That sounds great," Zach says. "I appreciate you taking us around and helping us to make an informed decision."

"Absolutely!" Ian says. "We're friends and I wouldn't want you to make a decision you and Emalee may regret."

They spend the afternoon with Foxy. "Let me tell you that, while this is paradise, it's not without its pitfalls. You, being from a coastal area, can appreciate the seasons we have. Tourist, slow and hurricane." Foxy chuckles. "If you decide to move forward with this venture, I'm sure that you will quickly learn the ins and out, along with the dos and the don'ts of island life. You are an outsider for a while. I am always here to provide you direction and counsel, should you need it."

Zach thanks him. They continue to discuss the nuances of the Virgin Islands for a while longer. They spend some time enjoying the sights and sounds of the bar. Zach and Emalee get a great deal of information, which they plan to use to make their decision about the Thirty Steps Inn.

"All right, crew. It's time to get back to Peter Island before I have anymore of Foxy's Punch and we're spending the night in the harbour on the hook. Let's load up and make the sail back," Ian announces.

Chapter 18

Morales and Espinoza work on reengineering the device into a weapon of some sort. Pierre is observing and reevaluating his alliance to Antonio Morales, his current mentor. Jean wants to create a better life for his people back in Haiti. Violent demonstrations and organized mayhem are not on his agenda. He knows the government of Haiti is corrupt. Can he change that? If the current administration is removed and exiled, will the next batch of political replacements be any better? Will they succumb to the temptations of money and power just like every leadership group since Jean-Claude Duvalier? Corruption has always been endemic in Haiti, but became much more widespread when its state finances were bankrupted under the rule of Jean-Claude "Baby Doc" Duvalier's regime from 1971 to 1986.

And it's been one crooked administration after the other. Along with the corruption is the widespread violence throughout the area of Port Au Prince. Murders, kidnapping for ransom, wide-ranging burglary and robbery. Even the cruise-line industry shies away from the country now, crushing its tourism industry.

No, if Jean Pierre is going to make a difference, he will have to do it not through violence but with innovation in order to improve the people's lives. Even if he has to do it one village at a time.

He tells Espinoza and Morales that he must return to Haiti to address an uprising in his village. "My comrade, Paul Baptiste, tells me there is a rival from the area stirring up trouble. You obviously don't need me here. I do not have the technical expertise to help you with the repurposing of that thing you're working on. I'll be back in a week."

With that, Jean Pierre makes his decision that working with this single-minded duo is not going to be his destiny. He closes the door to the warehouse building and walks to his waiting taxi, knowing he will not be returning to Cuba.

Morales watches as Jean Pierre leaves. He turns back to Espinoza, who is still tinkering with the Ben Burns Power Station. "So, do you think you'll be able to convert the inner working of this box into something with destructive capability?" Morales asks.

"I can't seem to make any sense of this. I'm going to have to open it up and take a look around the interior of the device," Espinoza responds. With that, he gathers some basic tools that most would have in a workbench in their garage. Craftsman screwdriver, wrench, pliers and hammer. Gently, he removes the outside panel of the device. Slowly, he removes the front panel and, at that moment, there is a low-pitched hum from inside. Morales and Espinoza duck for cover. The hum steadily increases in pitch, followed by a loud pop. That's it. A small plume of white smoke rises from the open unit. Morales and Espinoza peek over the desk they are hiding behind.

"What the hell?" Espinoza says.

"What happened?" Morales asks.

The two men with aspirations of making a bomb out of the stolen fusion device approach the open side of the unit. "It does appear that this small cube inside the unit is intact. I have to assume that it's the fuel cell. If it were compromised, I would expect we would have experienced more than a noise and a puff of smoke."

Espinoza cautiously pokes around with the screwdriver. "This is what powers the device. I recommend careful inspection. Decide if you can use it and if you can craft an explosive device with it and use a remote or timed detonation. If not, then I would think about ridding yourself of it. The rest of the thing, I don't' know what to think of it.

Whatever it may have been, it is no more. You should just chuck the box it came in into the ocean."

"I'll think about the disposal. If I can't utilize the fuel cell, maybe I can use it as a decoy, or maybe put a conventional bomb with remote detonation or a timer in it and still cause some commotion. We really just need to get the right people's attention. Once we have them listening, we can steal the money we need," Morales responds. "If I can't use the fuel cell, I'll make sure I get it to you for safekeeping."

"Where are you going to steal enough money to fund a revolution?" Espinoza asks derisively. "You need to buy guns and soldiers and equipment. If you have enough money, then people know you're serious. But that is a substantial amount, which you do not have."

"Grand Cayman is where the money is. It's close and the banks have plenty of money on hand, most legal some slightly dirty, if you catch my drift. You go back to Havana and let me devise a plan. I'll use the young Haitian rebel to plant the device and, if all goes wrong, he can take the fall." Morales grins. "I'll be in touch."

After Espinoza leaves the warehouse, Morales notices a tiny square on the outside of the fuel cell. With the help of a magnifying glass, he slowly works on the tiny piece. After what seems like an hour, he removes it very carefully with a razor's edge and fine-point tweezers. He puts it in a small bag and puts that inside a jar on the desk. Next, he begins carefully inspecting the fuel cell, making sure he didn't damage its casing. "That's all I need," he thinks to himself. "Too much to do to blow myself up today."

Chapter 19

Several months go by with few results in terms of finding treasure. Paul and Jackson find several coins and a few rings and necklaces but they are from the early twentieth century and not the early nineteenth, putting their finds in the wrong time frame. The tedious work of outlining the search grids, towing the magnetometers and employing the sub-floor sonar continues. They search the explorable water along the south side of Cayman Brac. Shawn studies the information obtained from NOAA concerning the tides and storms over the past several hundred years.

"It makes sense studying these and the other documentation as to why we are not finding much. Certainly, no trace of the Treasure of Lima. Let's go over the diary, the information that Jackson found in the archives in Seville, and the satellite imagery we were able to obtain. And a thank you to David Smith for the satellite photos."

David Smith, Alistair's best friend and close ally, always comes through with information or protection whenever it is needed. He is truly a key asset in this team's continuing adventures.

A few days ago the weather far to their east is beginning to churn. A small tropical low forms a few hundred miles east of the leeward islands in the Caribbean. "We can continue to search. Many times these storms amount to nothing or just move off in a different direction." Shawn says.

"Agreed," Captain Richard Jones says flatly. "However, I will watch her and continue to monitor the updates on her location, speed and projected path. For now, we'll continue our search."

Jackson, Shawn, Alistair, George, Scotty and Paul continue to take shifts. Two divers at a time in the water, one topside monitoring their progress and safety. The other three reviewing their findings, any anomalies from the magnetometer and sub-floor sonar, and mapping out their next search grid.

Time crawls along. Boredom is intermittently interrupted by a ping from the divers' detectors that indicate metal or iron. Unfortunately, they have found a few plane parts, some modern ship components, a few of the dive wrecks along the coast, but no cannons or bell or anything identifying the Treasure of Lima. As with any quality search, no matter what they find, they diligently make notes and mark the location of their anomaly.

Jackson says, "Let's go over again what I found in the General Archive of the Indies. There is not much on the *Mary Dear* or the Treasure of Lima. We'll have to continue to trust the diary and deathbed confession of John Keating. And so far, no luck with those."

"We still have the north side of Cayman Brac to search and possibly some areas toward Little

Cayman, if necessary. After that, we may need to review our strategy."

Hurricanes have a mind and a life of their own. Ask any weather-channel girl what a hurricane is going to do and they can give you a prediction, but the hurricane itself decides. Many are several hundred miles across and can do damage to a widespread area. Hurricane Hugo is a good example of a big hurricane doing damage to a massive geographic area. Some are small and develop a targeted punch. They can go from a tropical storm to a CAT 5 and back in a matter of a week. Penelope is no different. Just a few days ago, she was a tropical low bringing rain to the leeward islands. Now she's a CAT 4 skirting north of the Virgin Islands and Puerto Rico. Current path puts the southeastern tip of Cuba in the crosshairs of her wrath.

The search team makes a decision to suspend their operation until Penelope passes. Now the question is where they sail for safe harbor. The closest point of refuge is Grand Cayman but, given the current projected path, that might be robbing Peter to pay Paul. There is no guarantee Grand Cayman will be safe. Cuba is out of the question. Jamaica is possible and only two hundred nautical miles to Kingston on the south side. The *Marauder* is the slower of the boats and the *Migration* will follow. The thirty-foot Island Hopper flybridge dive boat, the Sea Hunt Gamefish 30, may be an issue. Crossing the open ocean may be risky and docking them at the port on Cayman Brac under the watchful eyes of the marina personnel may be their best option. It is a very small port located on the north side of the island, just about midpoint.

The Port of Kingston in Jamaica sits on the world's seventh-largest natural harbor. This port is on the strategic north/south-east/west axis across the Caribbean. It is approximately thirty-two miles away from the active trade routes that pass through the Panama Canal.

The only other viable option is Port Antonio. Port Antonio is the island's third-largest port, famous as a shipping point for mostly bananas and coconuts, and one of its most important tourist attractions. The city has been featured in major Hollywood films, like *Club Paradise, Cocktail* and James Bond films, and the Ken Wright Pier at the Errol Flynn Marina is the only one of Jamaica's cruise-ship ports. But it lies on the northern side of Jamaica and the storm could have a better chance of hitting there than Port Kingston to the south about sixty miles.

They make the arrangements and hunker down at the Port of Kingston for what they hope will only be a day or two, wanting to return to their search as soon as it is safe to sail.

As Shawn, Jackson and George head to shore to stock some food supplies and take as much water as is available, Jackson picks up a copy of the *Jamaica Observer* newspaper and begins browsing.

"Wait a minute," he shouts as he reads an article in the local news section. "This guy named Greg Wilson from Missouri found a coin while vacationing on Cayman Brac on the west end. They were staying at the Cayman Brac Resort. On his last day there, he found a coin among some other items in the sand. He didn't think much of it, he says, until he cleaned it. When he got back home to Missouri, he took it to a local coin dealer. The numismatist tells him he's found a gold doubloon, 8 Escudos, pure 22 karat, minted in Lima. Late 1700s. Says here the coin, in its current condition, is worth nearly three thousand dollars."

"What?" Shawn asks. "That's the time frame we're looking for! And he found it by metal detecting? On the beach? I can't wait until we get back to the site. Let's get back and tell the others about Mr. Wilson's find."

Chapter 20

Penelope was a small storm in terms of area, but a powerful hurricane. Only one hundred miles across with a twenty-mile-wide eye, she packed winds of one hundred forty miles per hour until making first landfall at Guantanamo Bay, Cuba, on that island's southwestern tip. She slowed slightly but hit the Caymans head on at one hundred and twenty-five miles per hour. A solid Cat 3 on the Saffir-Simpson Hurricane Wind Scale. She followed the Cayman Ridge and then headed on to Mexico, where she made a third landfall on the Yucatan Peninsula.

The Caymans are no stranger to dealing with the aftermath of hurricanes. The islanders are quick to clean up and repair and restore power. Clean-up this time follows a normal pattern. A few structures have been severely damaged but are repairable. Trees, palm fronds and sand have blown about and are blocking some right of ways. No loss of life has been reported on any of the three islands.

Rather than return straight to their search, the team instead turns to assisting islanders on Cayman Brac and Little Cayman with power and water restoration. Alistair has Virgin Power and Water ship five Ben Burns Power Stations via private charter plane to Grand Cayman, Little Cayman and Cayman Brac. They won't solve their big electrical issues but the first responders and residents will have some power and clean water until all services are restored on the islands.

Grand Cayman fairs better than her sister islands but does have some immediate power needs. After a week, life on Cayman Brac returns to relative normalcy, albeit with some secondary clean-up still to do.

The treasure seekers' small armada returns to the last search grid before evacuating prior to Hurricane Penelope's disruption. Shawn checks in with Sandra to make sure they faired the storm well and to see if she is having any luck with the sale of the Thirty Steps Inn.

Sandra says, "As a matter of fact, I heard from Zach and Emalee. While owning an inn in the Caribbean is something of a dream of Zach's, the timing is off. Zach owns three storefronts in the States and is opening a fourth. He and Emalee have just had their first child. Running the inn, even with the help from a local manager on site here, just seems a bit overwhelming at this point. They told me they appreciate the offer to buy, the hospitality and the tour of the area but they are not going to be able to purchase the Thirty Steps Inn."

"Well, damn. I was hoping you could find a buyer and then get over here and keep me company on these lonely nights at sea." Shawn smiles as he says it.

Sandra laughs out loud. "Oh, brother, is that the best line you've got? I thought you adventurers were the charmers. Anyway, as luck would have it, I found a potential buyer from neighboring St. Thomas. As you're well aware, local news and information is best spread over the coconut telegraph, the unwritten word-of-mouth and gossip communication system that is popular among islanders. So I put the word out. The buyer is Jane Sanders. She and her husband have a few small establishments in the tourist zone of St. Thomas and were very interested in obtaining the Thirty Steps Inn. Easiest real-estate transaction I've ever been a part of. A very straightforward and smooth deal, done in a day. My proceeds were sent to my account in the U.S. I made a little bit of money on the transaction and I'm satisfied both with the terms of the agreement and the new owners who are taking over the inn."

"That's great, babe. So when are you getting on a plane to come treasure hunt?" Shawn asks.

"Soon. Wait! Ian's right here and wants to say hi," Sandra says.

"Shawn!" Ian shouts into the phone. "It looks like we're open and free to come help you find the treasure you seek, my friend. Hannah, Sandra and I are ready if you need the help and if you have room for us."

"Of course we do, and we need some fresh eyes to look at this mountain of information and offer new perspectives on this search," Shawn replies.

Ian and Hannah dock the *Second Wind* at Great Harbour, where it can be looked after by Foxy and his able-bodied associates. Ian, Hannah and Sandra make arrangements to fly from St. Thomas to Miami to Cayman Brac. They decide to endure the marathon layover in Miami by visiting South Beach and enjoy the extremely overpriced beverages and dinner in the art-deco establishments.

After the crazy travel schedule and layovers, they arrive at Cayman Brac. They are met by a very happy Shawn, who has brought the dive boat to Cayman Brac Resort to collect his passengers.

"Ahoy!" Sandra shouts as she waves from the pier dock. She sprints to the dive boat and jumps into Shawn's waiting arms. "Been a long time," she whispers.

"Too long, Sandra. Too long," Shawn replies as they enjoy an extended kiss with each other.

"Okay, get a room!" Shawn shouts, and he and Hannah approach the interlocked couple. "Or at least a cabin."

They arrive and board the *Marauder*. After proper introductions with Jackson, Paul, Scotty and Richard, they shake hands and then give Alistair and George big hugs.

"So good seeing you all again," Alistair says. "It's been far too long. Last time we were together was the wedding."

"So how did you peel yourself away from Emma to come out here and search for a treasure that's supposed to be in another ocean?" Ian asks.

"Several things, actually. Emma is sequestered in London at Virgin Power and Water, working with their engineers and designers on the floating platforms. She also hasn't given up trying to adapt the Ben Burns Power Stations to inland communities. Rather than try to find a source other than sea water, she's working with Ethan, Aiden and others to find an economical, safe and practical way to move the seawater inland. They've gotten several prototypes of various pipeline designs utilizing various sizes of PVC piping."

"That's outstanding," Ian says. "She is one awesome individual. And is the pipeline system being tested now?"

"Yes, she has three she really likes but, based on the tests, her first design is the one functioning the most efficiently. We have great hope that it can be utilized for inland communities soon."

"So what did you have to bribe your new bride with so you could be diving in the Caribbean?"

"As it turns out, I promised I would take her to Montreux, Switzerland on Lake Geneva for a holiday. She loves Lake Geneva." Alistair laughs. "It might have been that incentive that allowed me this indulgence."

Chapter 21

Morales continues developing his plan, coming to the conclusion that an old-fashioned remedy to the situation is the best course of action. He decides that using conventional explosives and encasing the fuel cell with them will provide proper explosive power.

"I don't know how to trigger the fusion cell directly," he ponders. "So a chain reaction, C-4 triggers the fusion cell, and I should get the explosion I want to get the attention of the bank." He marvels with ill intent at the metal box. He has taken it to the seaside in Puerto Padre more than once to rent a boat and toss it in the ocean. But something won't let him. He thinks it is admiration for those that developed this seemingly simple, yet vastly complicated unit.

In addition to the modified fusion-cell explosive device, Morales feels he needs another device. One for a diversion, allowing him to threaten the bank and detonate the fusion cell after the money is transferred to him.

Traditional bomb-making is tricky. The builder needs to use non-detectable explosives and a timing device or a remote detonator. Do it wrong and you could blow yourself up. Patience and know-how are key. Morales has made his share of these for all sorts of mercenaries, rebellions and governments, including his own. Many of them have ended up in parts of the world where no one really cares about a bomb going off and news of such incidents is suppressed. Some he's used to disrupt military operations or utilities. Some for kidnapping and ransom. Others he's used in city centers, where the objective is to get a bank or financial institution to give you, or transfer to an account, a great deal of money. That is the purpose for this creation.

Morales thinks to himself as he works on his devices, "Jean Pierre, the Haitian, trying to be a rebel who doesn't like violence. How can that be? How can you

lead a rebellion without some sort of firepower?"
Jean Pierre left for Haiti over a month ago. He has contacted Morales on two occasions to explain why he hasn't returned to assist. Just a few days ago, Jean made his last call to Morales. He went on to explain that, while he was very appreciative of Morales' interest and initial support, their ideas of rebellion are decidedly different. He is opting out of Morales' plan and will work on finding peaceful solutions to his cause. He tells Morales that he will not be assisting him in Grand Cayman or anywhere else.

Jean Pierre decides another course of action. He will contact a man whose name he overheard when he and Morales stole the power station in Acklins. Foxy Caldwell is the name. Morales told Pierre that his contact at Soper's Hole on Tortola tipped him off regarding the exploits of Mr. Caldwell. Morales went on to say there were rumors circulating that he has, or knows of, a device that not only creates electrical power but also, as a by-product, produces clean water through the use of a small fusion reactor.

After it became clear to Jean that Morales and Espinoza were going to use destruction force as their primary method of rebellion, Pierre decided there might be another way. If he could speak to Mr. Caldwell—and if there is such a device—then Pierre could bring it to the poverty-stricken people of his land and give them electricity and water. He and others could teach them how to use these tools for farming, for hygiene, and to create a better way of life.

Foxy is wary at first, and he contacts Alistair to inform him that Jean Pierre is reaching out to him. He explains that Jean was with the man who stole the device at Acklins and almost killed John Campbell. "Do you know where the stolen power station is currently?" Foxy asks.

"Still showing its location in the same warehouse district in Puerto Pardre, Cuba," Alistair responds.

"Just be careful and use your best judgment," Alistair advises.

"I'm a pretty good judge of people I don't know or have just met," Foxy tells Alistair. "I know there are nefarious people out there, but something inside tells me that Jean Pierre is really trying to do positive things. He told me that the man who recruited him—a Cuban by the name of Antonio Morales—would have killed John Campbell. But Jean intervened. And he contacted me regarding the Ben Burns Power Station—the box, as he calls it. He heard rumors that it could produce power and clean water and he thinks that is exactly the type of asset that can help his people out of poverty and continued dependence on a corrupt system."

"I trust your judgment, Foxy," Alistair replied. "Just keep me posted on the situation. I'd like to meet this young man. Make sure to check in after your meeting so I know you're safe, and you can give me your assessment after meeting this Jean Pierre face-to-face. I'm in Cayman Brac but can get a plane to Grand Cayman fairly quickly and then to Tortola or St. Thomas."

Meanwhile, back in Puerto Padre...

It takes the better part of a month but Antonio Morales develops his plan and builds the devices he plans to deploy. He calls his contacts on Grand Cayman that he has employed over the years. He is a master at bribery and convincing lower- to mid-level workers that his cause is just. Providing them with a cash bonus for looking the other way or moving a questionable package through is easy money and an invaluable resource for Morales.

In reality, he isn't sure he even believes his rhetoric. He is greedy just like the next person. He likes the money. Since Jean Pierre has bowed out, he can go forward with his plan to pilfer large sums from the Cayman National Bank, to line his pockets and fund his account in Switzerland, and leave Cuba. He wants to use the bank in Nassau, Bank of the

Bahamas, which he has used in the past and where he maintains an account in another name with a modest balance. However, banks in this part of the world tend to keep close tabs on illegal activity, including ransom and robbery. They don't really care about the activity of their customers so much; they just want to protect their assets. A theft or an unusually large money transfer from the largest bank on Grand Cayman would send a heads up to the other banks in the Caribbean. Stealing money in the Caymans and moving it directly to Nassau would create an investigation The receiving Bank of the Bahamas would likely feel an obligation to freeze and eventually return the cash.

His plan is to ship the incendiary devices to the Grand Caymans through customs. They are not assembled but all the components are in three separate containers. One of his contacts is a supervisor on the island. He has identified the crates as tourist brochures printed off island and shipped to the Bureau of Tourism. Morales specifically informs the supervisor of the unique markings on the outside of the crates so they will be readily identifiable by the customs official. They will then be cleared and stored until Morales collects them and pays the supervisor his standard bribery fee.

He makes a reservation at the five-star Ritz Carlton on Seven Mile Beach. Morales originally planned to make the Ritz Carlton his first target, but he has now chosen to target Cayman National Bank, with both devices placed in strategic locations within the building to make the greatest impact. Obviously, an explosion at the Ritz Carlton would bring unwanted attention in terms of investigators and thwart his plan for the bank. His plan is to create chaos, with dust and debris flying around, people running in all directions, alarms and sirens. The works, so to speak. He has no plans to intentionally injure or kill anyone, but it is certainly likely to happen and will not weigh on his conscious.

He studies the blueprints of the bank provided by his contacts inside. He scours the drawings and notes the management offices, the vault, and where the security is centered. He selects where he wants to plant each bomb at Cayman National. His two contacts who work maintenance for the bank are dedicated to their own financial wellbeing and ready to assist. Morales promises them he will give them proper handguns to rob the teller cages, creating even more mayhem. This will provide Morales with an additional diversion to get his money transferred.

Morales is not going to take any money from the teller line. He'll leave that to his two cohorts. He also doesn't need to get the manager to open the safe so he can rifle through their precious cache of safe deposit boxes of the rich and ruthless.

The first bomb will be placed in a discrete area near the safe. This should create enough of a panic that the safe is the target. Once he has the attention of the manager, he will explain that a second, much larger device will detonate should the bank senior manager not immediately wire his money. Once the transfer is made to his Swiss account, he will exit the bank through the maintenance area. Once outside, he'll press a four-digit code into his cell phone to detonate the second device in the third-floor offices. He could ask for a hundred million because the bank has that kind of capital. He's only going for ten million. He figures that is enough to retire in style and get out of the Caribbean for good. He plans to leave the mundane life he has established in his native Cuba. Tired of the strain of living in a failing dictatorship. Maybe a small place in Greece. A great climate and on the Mediterranean. That will be a much better life.

He goes back to the plan and reviews it again and again. After he is comfortable with the layout, he turns his attention to the timing of it all. Once he has gotten his route inside the bank memorized, he turns his attention to making contact with his maintenance duo to review the plan with them. He has to make sure they know what to do and where to be at the precise time. He only has one chance at this and it has to be carried out with precision.

Chapter 22

The treasure team continues the methodical search for any indication of treasure. They want to jump over to the spot where Greg Wilson found the Spanish doubloon on the beach at the west end. Jackson cautions, "You know we need to continue this search in a very methodical way. That coin could have been swept over years ago from this spot we're anchored on. Steady as we go."

Of course, the others reluctantly agree. Scotty and Jackson are the first to dive, and Shawn and Sandra monitor their status from the deck of the dive boat. As they resume searching their virtual grid, they notice that the seafloor has been transformed by Hurricane Penelope. She was not wide, as storms go, but she packed a powerful punch, much like Andrew did in the 1990s to the southeast Florida coast.

"There must be twenty feet of overburden and rock that has been washed away by the storm," Scotty reports to Shawn. "We need to deploy the sub-floor sonar immediately. What we didn't find twenty feet below the surface before Penelope, we may find twenty feet below the new seafloor level. Essentially, we can see forty feet down now."

In the meantime, Ian and Hannah go to the west end and the Cayman Brac Resort to snoop around the beach with some metal detectors. One for land and one for use in the shallow water near the beach. They all agree that they don't need everyone at once on the boats and it certainly can't hurt to have a look at the beach where the doubloon was recovered. Ian and Hannah check in at the resort and go right to work with their surface search. They scour the beach during the day and catalog and examine any of their finds by night. They don't find a great deal the first few days. Typical metal-detection finds, including bottle caps, some American quarters and dimes, a British pound coin. There is a slim gold chain, white-gold men's wedding ring and a fork. Too modern and definitely not a treasure trove by any stretch. On the next to last day of their stay at the resort, Ian takes his snorkel gear and the water-safe metal detector for a swim around the shallows. Hannah stays on the beach near the water's edge conducting her own sweeping search. She has learned from Ian how to search with the metal detector in a visual grid without missing any area. Ian marks a one-hundred-yard long search area, estimating the distance from a lone coconut palm at one end of the beach to two giant fan palms at the other end. His depth will be ankle deep to ten feet putting his search-area width at about twenty yards. Hannah stays near the water's edge to conduct her own sweeping search of the beach. She learns from Ian how to search with the metal detector using a grid laid out in her mind without any gaps. She focuses on an area further away from their previous search.

After a long afternoon of searching, they are rewarded. In about four feet of water, not quite a foot under the sand, a gold coin, the number four on it and a mint date of 1715. Not far from where this coin is found, a small black blob registers a hit. Ian puts that in his bag with the coin. He marks the spot with his GPS locator and goes ashore to find Hannah.

Back in their room, Ian says, "I can't believe I found this. A México four escudos from 1715. See the date is partially obscured but that is seven one five and the first number must be a one. Definitely gold. But where did this little item come from? Our ship went down in the early 1800s. Then there's this little black blob that is very likely a cluster of coins. Because of the color, it very well may be silver coin."

"Tomorrow after checkout, we need to go straight to the *Marauder*," Hannah says. "We need to verify with Jackson and the group what we found and, more importantly, where we found them. Could they be from the Treasure of Lima?"

"The date on the gold coin is puzzling to say the least. It is a gold coin from 1715. Let's pack up so we can get out of here at dawn."

Ian thinks to himself, "What is a coin from 1715 doing on a ship from the 1800s?"

Chapter 23

"It's a Mexico four escudos from 1715," Jackson says flatly. "Look at the markings. These indicate where it was minted." He points out the detail with his index finger. "You are correct on the date."

Alistair says, "Is that possibly from the ship we're looking for? Is that a possibility?"

Jackson replies, "Anything's possible but, normally, the dates should coincide with the date of the wreck. Our ship went down around 1820 after the Spanish left Lima due to the uprising. This coin is over a hundred years before then." And then something clicked. "Wait a minute. I'll be right back!"

A few minutes later, Jackson returns with his laptop and binder of paper files. "Here! When I was in Seville the last time, I was going through the archives trying to find any additional information on the *Mary Dear, La Senora de Colon* and the Treasure of Lima. I also searched through the records for anything related to the Caymans, and particularly Little Cayman and Cayman Brac, since that's the geographical description that the diary and some other documents indicate. While in Spain, I ran across this." He shows them a part of a diary, wrapped in seal skin, which was recovered on Little Cayman in the early eighteenth century. "It refers to the *Nuestra Senora de Madeira*. She was part of a 1730 Spanish treasure fleet. She sailed undercover as a cargo ship but she was covertly a treasure ship. According to the captain's diary, the *Nuestra Senora de Madeira* carried one hundred thousand gold doubloons and two hundred thousand silver coins, along with emeralds and other precious stones. There is also mention of a cache of emeralds of varying size and a hammered gold chalice. According to the log filed as he left Havana, the ship was carrying simple cargo. His diary obviously tells another story. The captain was to deliver the ship to the Port of Seville."

"So, the coin that Ian found could possibly be from that ship?" Shawn asks excitedly. "Holy smokes! Let's review what little we have. Greg Wilson finds a coin minted in Peru with a mint date of 1798. Ian finds a coin from Mexico with a mint date of 1715 in nearly the same spot. Are we looking at two wrecks next to each other a hundred years apart?"

Alistair says, "Sure seems like that could be the case."

Jackson says, "I know that we were going to move methodically down the north side of the island east to west. If we continue as we have, we'll be at the south end of the island in one week."

"Let's roll with it. If the treasure is there, it isn't going anywhere in a week," Richard Jones, the captain, says.

They agree to continue the search. Days go by with little to no excitement or discovery of any valuable artifacts. They find more remnants of more modern sunken boats and planes used to create a reef and used as dive sites for the tourists. The more recognized of these purposely sunken boats is the MV *Captain Keith Tibbetts*. Located on the northern side and near the western tip of the island, the wreck of the *Keith Tibbetts* is a popular dive site in Cayman Brac. Sunk intentionally in 1996, this Russian destroyer was given to Cuba, who sold it to the Caymans specifically to serve as an artificial reef. The ship is approximately 330 feet (100 meters) long, and the shallow depth allows amateur divers to stay down longer.

The *Marauder* divers find other interesting artifacts, including some shards of pottery and urns, but not much more. The pottery and urn pieces look like they could be from the proper time period. They bag several pieces to run a test. Typical testing include carbon-14 or optically stimulated luminescence. Neither of which they have on hand. Alistair says he'll get it to a lab as soon as possible.

A week goes by and they are at the site of the two gold coins found by Greg Wilson and Ian Marshall.

"The black blob you found is, in fact, silver coins. I have them in a chemical solution now so we can determine time frame and origin," Jackson says. "Silver coins, when found in the ocean, will have an encrustation that is typically blackish in color. This is because salt water corrodes silver. And any artifact found in salt water has to initially stay in salt water until it is conserved. Taking it out of the salt water and exposing it to the air results in a highly accelerated decomposition. It can literally crumble away before your eyes. Both mechanical and chemical methods are used to remove encrustation. Gold coins, on the other hand, do not corrode in salt water, and if they have encrustation, it will typically be greenish in color. Once we remove the encrustation, the coins are pretty much in the same condition as they were when they went down with the ship. Problem is that copper and bronze artifacts can also have a greenish color encrustation.

So you don't really know what you have until the encrustation is removed."

"What are you soaking them in?" Shawn asks.

"It's a basic solution I've used many times before with an acetone base. Then I transfer them to a solution of baking soda, lemon juice and some club soda. It doesn't clean them completely, but it will let us know what we're dealing with until we can get them a proper bath," Jackson explains. "We should know what we have in the silver coins in a few hours."

Other boats are in the area. Mostly curiosity seekers taking an interest in the seventy-foot plus *Marauder* and the dive activity going just offshore. However, there is one particular vessel a little farther away than the other onlookers. The forty-two-foot Auroris Cigarette observes the small treasure armada from a comfortable distance. "What are they doing now?" says Julio Álvarez, who is manning the helm.

"Just continuing to dive. There isn't a lot of activity. They seem to have found a few items but nothing worth stealing. We should wait to see if they come up with some real treasure," replies Estefan Gomez peering through the long-range binoculars. "In fact, they may be calling it a day for now."

"Let's head on back to Little Cayman so we can refuel and check in with our contacts in Haiti and Puerto Padre," orders Julio.

Back in Puerto Padre...

Morales continues to work on the plan to obtain his retirement money from the Cayman National Bank. He has already made the decision to give up on Jean Pierre. The pacifist has no idea how to lead a revolution or what's involved. "He would have been a hinderance to my plans anyway," thinks Morales. A few days after Jean Pierre left Cuba, Morales is contacted by a rouge by the name of Julio Álvarez. Álvarez has heard through village gossip that Jean Pierre was working with a Cuban national by the name of Antonio Morales who had planned to plant explosive devices and rob a bank in Grand Cayman.

"Paul Baptiste, Jean Pierre's number-two man-had told a few people he was recruiting for the *Libérer Haiti* revolution. The information was passed to me and I thought we should make contact."

"And who might you be, and why exactly are you contacting me?" Morales asks emphatically.

"Julio Álvarez. I run a small, but very profitable, pirating operation out of Les Cayes in southwestern Haiti. We operate throughout the Caribbean and we focus our efforts on the very rich tourists and their assets, as opposed to hijacking freighters and cargo ships, although we are not opposed to pirating them if the right opportunity presents itself."

Piracy in the Caribbean is not as rampant as in its past, nor as widespread as it has been on the west African coast, specifically, Somalia. But it does exist. Primarily, the country of Venezuela has been a haven for modern piracy in the area. And, unlike in the golden age of piracy, there are no three-mast galleons captained by Blackbeard or Calico Jack with their band of savage pirates on board. Today, the piracy is conducted in fast powerboats, mainly Cigarette models or similar makes operated by three or four heavily armed bandits who board ships and take whatever valuables are on board. On rare occasions, they may kidnap the occupants of the vessel or simply hold them hostage for ransom. They tend to stay away from the areas where the U.S. Coast Guard and British Royal Navy conduct regular patrols and have maritime jurisdiction.

"Once again, why are you contacting me?" Morales fumes.

Álvarez explains what he knows in detail. Then he says, "If you're interested in joining forces, so to speak, we might make quite the score in terms of gold and silver."

"I'm listening." Morales hears the caller's proposal and the possible windfall. "So they haven't found anything of great value as yet. And we don't know the ship for which they are searching. Sounds like a stretch. But I'm always willing to listen. Where would you like to meet?"

"I can be there in a day. I'm currently in Little Cayman and I'll meet you at Manzanillo. We'll grab lunch. I'm bringing three men with me. We will be armed, just so you are aware," Álvarez says.

"I will be traveling alone and I, too, will be armed to level the playing field. Come to the Bahia de Caimanera and moor there. I'll meet you at Chantilly on Avenida Juárez and Madero Centro, where we can have lunch and discuss our future endeavor together," Morales says. "You will need papers to enter Cuba from the sea. Do you have proper documentation for entry."

Álvarez laughs. "Yes, Señor Morales. We have documentation. We are not only pirates; we are also very good at forging documents. Additionally, since we have pirated tourists over the past several years, we've stolen their papers, passports and boat registrations, so we know exactly what the governments in the Caribbean require for entry."

"I'll see you tomorrow at Chantilly. If you don't show, I'll know you're not who you say you are, or that you have no backbone, like your fellow countryman." Morales says as he hangs up the phone.

Chapter 24

Alistair informs the group that Foxy has been contacted by one of the people involved in the ambush of John Campbell and the theft of the Ben Burns Power Station from Acklins. The man's name is Jean Pierre. The unit that was stolen is still tracking to a warehouse in Puerto Padre. So nothing has changed there. The unit has either been dismantled and shut itself down, or the thief gave up trying to copy it or use it in some other nefarious manner.

"I've had my close contacts run some background on him. There's not a lot on him. Twenty-nine, native of Belladere in the mountains of Haiti bordering Elias Pina in the Dominican Republic. He started what amounts to a ragtag assemblage of disgruntled locals who want a better life for their families. There are maybe thirty males of similar age that make up the group. They call themselves

Libérer Haiti. There has been no violence perpetrated by their group. They appear to be trying to find solid footing in terms of financing and ideology, but have had no measured success with either," Alistair says.

"I'm planning on meeting him," Foxy responds. "I want to meet in St. Thomas, away from Tortola or Jost, in case there are any prying eyes about. I'll arrange a meeting on St. Thomas, say, a week from today. I think it will benefit all of us to have a face to face meeting. We'll listen to this man and see if he is legitimately interested in peacefully helping his people."

"George and I will be there to meet with you and Mr. Pierre," Alistair replies. "Meet us at the Emerald Beach Bar just down from the airport. I'll be there in a week. I look forward to seeing you again. In fact, I'll plan on staying an extra day and we can get caught up on the goings on in the area and review our thoughts on Mr. Pierre."

Back in Belladere...

Jean Pierre meets with his small group of rebels. He says to the group, "Killing and bombing and mayhem is not how I see helping our people. The Cuban national who I met and spent time with, along with one of his government confidantes, is laser focused on violence. It doesn't have to be that way. We need to show our people that we can overcome our circumstances through hard work, education and innovation."

"What are you talking about," shouts one of the men in the back of the room. "How can we overcome this oppression without the use of force? The government and police won't listen to us. They'll destroy us."

"Ah, but that's where we may have an option that no one has thought of, and that includes me until a few short days ago," Jean responds. "Let me explain to you what I have discovered in my visit to Cuba, the Bahamas, and back again."

Jean goes on to explain to the group that there is a device that uses something called nuclear fusion. "I have only started researching the concept. But there is a group of scientists who have developed a box that creates electricity from seawater, and its byproduct is clean water."

"That's crazy!" from someone in the back.

"There's no way that such a thing exists, Jean Pierre. You're lying to us!" Another yells.

"Have you seen this box work? Have you seen with your own eyes the power and water it produces?" Another questions from the front.

"I have seen the box. I have held it in my hands and I have touched it. I have not seen it work. I do know that it was important enough for me and Morales, the Cuban, to take an eight-hour round-trip boat ride from Puerto Padre in Cuba to Acklins in the Bahamas. Morales nearly killed the proprietor and might have had I not intervened. He wanted the box because he felt the fuel that made it work could be repurposed into a nuclear detonation device. Needless to say, after weeks of trying and tinkering with the device, he failed. In fact, the box just died. Quietly and without detonating or any other destructive measure," Jean explains to the group.

Paul Baptiste, one of the cooler heads in the room, asks, "So what makes you think the box does what you say it can?"

"Prior to us stealing the box from Acklins, one of Morales' confidantes on Tortola told him of a man who was using one of these in the area. I recalled the name and made contact with him. He is willing to meet with me at his home on Jost Van Dyke. I explained to him who I am and why I am interested in it; that I represent a group trying to lead a peaceful rebellion to improve the conditions of the poverty stricken in Haiti."

"And he agreed to this meeting? You are going?" Baptiste asks.

"I am going to St. Thomas in a few days to determine what exactly the box I saw is capable of and then I will see what we need to do in order to get a box. Think about the possibilities if it's true. Giving our village electricity! Having clean water to not only use for sanitation but to irrigate crops and drink without fear of disease," Jean says with excitement.

Chapter 25

On a bright, sunny day in the old town center of Manzanillo, two unsavory characters meet at the Chantilly Manzanillo Café. They order two *cervezas* and an order of *enfrijolodas,* a Mexican dish made of corn tortillas and bean sauce stuffed with cheese and onions. Also, an order of *Camarones a la Diabla,* large shrimp covered in a bright-red chili-pepper sauce. The tiny café is nearly empty so they speak freely.

"Why do you want to try and steal money from a bank using a bomb? You're wiring the money so trying to threaten them with explosives is simply overdoing it. You need to rethink that. Either hack their banking system and steal the money remotely or just give up on that pipedream. Robbing a bank. Sheesh. You'll just end up dead." Alvarez half sneers at Morales.

"I've made the decision to get out of Cuba. I want to go to Europe, probably Greece or Crete. I could stand the climate there and I could live very well on the money I was planning to steal," Morales snarls back. "What's your big plan of action?"

"So funding the revolution is out?" Alvarez laughs as he asks the question.

"The *Libérer Haiti* are on their own. I never really cared anyway. The kid, Jean Pierre, didn't have the heart to carry out a rebellion. He certainly couldn't help me, the Cuban government, or our allies. So, yes, I don't really care about that. I do care about my early retirement and a long, prosperous life of leisure."

"Okay then. Let's look at another option that can provide prosperity for both of us. And not get us blown up by one of your homemade bombs," Alvarez says. "Let's discuss the piracy option. There are four small ships anchored off the west end of Cayman Brac. We've had them under surveillance for a couple of weeks. They're on to something because they've been anchored in relatively the same position for the past week. They are consistently raising dive baskets from the ocean floor. They are in about seventy feet of water. They dive for a couple of hours at a time, two divers at a time. They have some contraption that looks like an oddly shaped stingray, which they take down at least twice a day. I don't think they've found any big score but there is a great deal of excitement at times on deck when emptying the contents of the dive baskets."

"You have my attention, to say the least," Morales responds. "Do you have any idea what wreck they're searching for?"

"No, and I don't care. Gold and silver is valuable, whether it's from the 1700s or last year. I just want to put a bunch of it on our boat and then we can divide it amongst ourselves." Alvarez continues, "We need to do some calculations on weight of coins and anything else of value. I assume we'll get one chance at plunder, and the last thing we want to do is overload a vessel that we're using to get away."

"Why would we try and transfer the loot not knowing how much it weighs or how much they have on board? Are we holding them at gunpoint while we methodically load our boat? Are we stealing the ship? Doesn't sound like you've thought this through. Robbing the bank seems like a more prudent idea compared to your plan," Morales says.

"A one-ounce pure-gold coin is worth twenty-five hundred dollars. Sixteen coins is a pound and you get forty thousand dollars. That doesn't include the intrinsic value of it being a shipwreck coin. But just sticking to the market value, two hundred and fifty pounds of gold coins gets you your ten million. Double it and I'll take the other ten million," Alvarez says. "We're not talking about a lot of weight. We just need to know that they have it on board. For the time being, we'll continue to watch and learn what they've found and where on the big boat they're storing the coins."

"It seems too complicated and extremely inefficient. Let's say you take the big boat and subdue the crew. Then you transfer up to five hundred pounds of gold from the big boat—and you're assuming it's there and hasn't been transported already. Finally, you're going to try and get away by sea-lugging that extra weight with God knows who's chasing you." Morales argues. "You can't get away with that."

Alvarez says, "I've done this for several years. You'd be very surprised by the power in those Cigarette boat engines. We're talking about the same cargo weight as hauling a couple of huge fish. It can be done." He speaks confidently but even he knows he has moved five hundred pounds on his boat at top speed. "You coming with us?"

"No, I'm going to fly into Grand Cayman and proceed with my plan of robbing the bank. In case either one of our individual plans fails or is compromised, keep your cell phone handy and I'll do the same. I'll look forward to seeing you there."

"Hoping we have a prosperous but limited partnership, Mr. Morales."

"Same goes for me, Mr. Alvarez. Same goes for me."

Chapter 26

Alistair meets with Foxy and Jean in St. Thomas at the Emerald Beach Bar, just a half-mile from Cyril E. King Airport, as planned. Alistair and George rise when they see Foxy. "Foxy, so good to see you again!" Alistair says, giving Foxy a friendly embrace.

"Alistair, it is good to see you too. I see that you have been enjoying the sunshine and staying fit." Foxy smiles. "This is the young man I have been telling you about. Jean Pierre, meet Alistair James."

"It's a pleasure to meet you, Mr. James," Jean says and extends his hand.

"Likewise, Mr. Pierre. I look forward to our conversation today," Alistair replies. "George, we'll be sitting by the railing overlooking the bay. You're welcome to join us."

"Thank you, Mr. James. I would prefer to take a seat over there so I can keep an eye on the entire bar," George replies, pointing to a stool near the end of the bar.

"Very well, then. We may be a while," Alistair says.

George nods and walks his large muscular frame over to the stool he indicated. Always dressed in black, ever vigilant about the goings on around his friend, Alistair.

The other three huddle at the table by the railing. They engage in a brief general conversation and then they get to the reason they're there. Foxy starts by explaining the entire situation of delivering, setting up and testing the Ben Burns Power Station on Acklins. He showed John "Bonefisher" Campbell how to run and maintain the unit. "Then I left and flew back home."

Jean Pierre goes next. He tells his story, starting with the formation of *Libérer Haiti.* He explains how he had been contacted by the Cuban, Antonio Morales, who offered to help him with his efforts to lead a rebellion. "Mr. Morales uses a single-minded approach to my cause. Destruction. I am not in favor of that. I got my first insight into this man's demeanor when he took me to Acklins to steal the power unit." Jean goes on to explain how Morales was going to kill John Campbell until Pierre stopped him. "Then we went back to Puerto Padre, where he and another Cuban, a friend of his, Renaldo Espinoza, attempted over the course of many days to find the fuel source, the fusion source, as they attempted to create an explosive device from it. Needless to say, they failed." He explains that he is not going to be involved in their bombmaking operation and that he decided to leave Cuba and go back to Haiti. "Before I left Cuba, I made a phone call to Mr. Caldwell here and asked him for a meeting. I couldn't say much over the phone at the airport but implored him I needed to see him. He agreed and I took the next flight from Puerto Pardre to Tortola."

"That's an interesting tale, Mr. Pierre. I am here to take this meeting with you based on Mr. Caldwell's recommendation for me to do so. I have spoken to him and he assures me that you are on the level and you seem to sincerely regret the Acklins incident, along with ever getting involved with Antonio Morales."

"Alistair, I know we've had issues with people in our recent past, but I'm confident Jean Pierre is nothing like what we've had to deal with," says Foxy. "In addition, he wants to help his people in ways to improve their standard of living. He reminds me of myself, wanting to help and trying to protect the people of Jost Van Dyke."

Alistair says, "Okay, Mr. Pierre. Please tell me what it is you are wanting from us."

Jean Pierre then tells Alistair and Foxy about his background, his village and the poverty they are forced to endure. He continues to tell Alistair that, if there really is a power station and it really does produce electricity and provide clean water, then he can transform the village to an independent and growing concern. Jean proceeds to explain his vision.

"With the electricity, we can provide a safe space for our children and elders. We can run generators and equipment, build sound structures for housing and education, and build food storage. With the water, I dream of creating an agricultural village where we can grow our own produce and fruits without having to purchase them elsewhere if we can find them available."

"That's admirable, certainly," Alistair responds. "The development of our unit, or box, as you have said, was to help those that aren't being served by big utilities or are in small population centers where the utility companies can't justify building the infrastructure. That said, I do have some concern over your association with a Cuban national with government contacts who is a bombmaker. Again, please tell me how you became associated with this individual."

Jean Pierre, once again, calmly and in detail, describes how the association began and how he, Jean, put an end to it.

"I will accept your explanation. Foxy has said that he believes you to be true and a kindred spirit of sorts with your desire to help others. Now, let's have a look at where you're located and what obstacles we may face in trying to get the water to you," Alistair states. He removes his laptop from its carrying case and opens it on the table just as the lunch arrives. They continue their discussion while enjoying the local fish tacos and the golden-brown conch-fritter appetizers.

"Belladere is up in the mountains near the border with the Dominican Republic, far away from the sea. Our device, that we now call the Ben Burns Power Station, can only be powered by seawater. So our challenge is to pump the seawater from the coast to your village. We're working on a piping system as we speak to divert the seawater inland so the benefits of it may be delivered to more areas than just coastal communities or islands. Foxy, have you tried the piping system that the team's been developing?"

"We've had some success in running the pipe to an area further inland on Jost. The water flow has been reaching the additional unit Ethan and Aiden provided for us. It's only been a few weeks but everything seems to be functioning normally," Foxy explains.

"That's excellent. Now let's look at the logistics of how we're going to run your pipeline to your village," Alistair says.

"One other issue. Remember the government of Haiti is corrupt. Also, there may be those who do not wish for us to have the product of electricity and water and would destroy it. We have good relations with those just on the other side of the border with the Dominican Republic. They might be willing to assist us," Jean Pierre says. "I'll go back and make contacts with the few villages that we would need to run the piping through."

"That's great information. Let's get to work and determine material needs, and you make some contacts with the villagers on the Dominican side."

With that, they shake hands and depart the establishment.

A few hours later...

Alistair and George fly from St. Thomas to Nassau so they can pick up the Cessna he has kept there since selling Cave Cay. Having it there makes it easy to get to Jost Van Dyke and to Necker Island if needed. The Cessna 208 Caravan is excellent for carrying people or cargo. The Cessna 208 is a high-wing braced-cabin monoplane powered by a single Pratt & Whitney turboprop. The cabin has room for nine passengers and two crew when used as a passenger aircraft. The aircraft can be optionally fitted with an underslung cargo pod.

Alistair added the adaptation of floats with retractable landing gear, this giving him the option of using either the runway or the water for takeoff and landing.

"We'll get the plane checked out and then you and I will fly it back to Cayman Brac airport. When we find the gold, we may need it to transport some of the treasure," Alistair says to George with a laugh.

Alistair and George check in at a fine establishment on Cable Beach away from the carnival over on Paradise Island. He arranges a secure Zoom meeting so he can meet with Emma, Ethan and Aiden regarding the situation in Haiti and the development of the pipeline, along with other issues.

Alistair provides his team in Colchester with the details of his meeting with Jean Pierre. He explains that this may be the true calling of Ben Burns Power Station—to help truly impoverished people in areas where assistance is lacking or non-existent.

The group agrees and signs off to get to work.

Chapter 27

In the meantime, the ocean is reluctant to give up the motherlode. Gold coins here and there and some unique gold chains. They continue to on board their finds and record each item and the location where it was found. A couple of weeks go by and then they find a coin. Then another and another. However, the coins' mint dates are a hundred years apart.

The Cayman government keeps a watchful eye on the treasure hunters. Not wanting to miss out on a windfall, they keep close tabs and insist that Alistair and his group record, document and report to the officials in the government offices of Historical Resources, Environment, and Coast Works. The government agrees to allow the ecological dredging and removal of certain artifacts. Any monetary value claimed by the James dive group is commissioned at twenty percent to the Cayman Islands. They have also agreed that numismatic experts from England, Spain and the United States will be used to assess value. Assets other than coin will be valued in a similar fashion by experts in their field.

The original permits provided for twelve months of exploration and dredging and recovery of items. The time for renewal is approaching and Shawn will be visiting the required departments early to ensure uninterrupted exploration.

Chapter 28

Alvarez continues to monitor the onloading to the *Marauder* from the divers. It is nearly nonstop. He has counted the number of items, be they boxed or in collection bags, that have been taken on board. He just doesn't know what's in them. From this distance, he cannot tell. Nine people are on board. They still have the three other vessels. The dive boat is used the most, then the Sea Hunt 380 for towing the search devices. The last boat, a large catamaran, is apparently being utilized for accommodations and transport. Alvarez is unaware that it also has a Ben Burns Power Station providing the group with power and water.

During daylight, there are several pleasure craft in the area—curious onlookers—but at night, there are no other boats visible. Alvarez tells his three fellow pirates that they will board and attach the ship at night. "We'll subdue the crew and then load the treasure. No casualties, if possible, but there are circumstances where that may be the only course of action."

The other three all nod in agreement. They have all done this before.

"Now get some rest," Alvarez orders. "We'll wait and watch to see what else they bring up before we go in. Then we'll get some of that treasure they've found."

Meanwhile, on Grand Cayman...

"Thank you," Morales tells the guest clerk at the Ritz Carlton. "Room 525, did you say?" The desk clerk affirms the room number. "No, these are the only bags I have. I won't be needing a bellman."

Normally, Morales isn't as pleasant in his dealings with anyone but he figures being nice to the staff won't draw attention to himself. Being a jerk certainly will, though. He checks in and, with his brand new satellite phone, calls his contact, the Customs supervisor.

"This is Antonio Morales. Did the tourism brochures arrive? Yes, good. When can I pick them up from Customs? Ten tomorrow morning? Excellent."

He will use his two maintenance contacts at the bank and place both devices in separate locations within the bank. But today, he will go to the bank, enter maintenance and obtain a uniform from his contacts. Then they will perform routine maintenance in all areas of the bank, simulating a typical workday. If asked, the third guy is a new hire and is in training.

Once he completes a physical walkthrough and gets a visual feel of the layout, he will determine the best places to hide the bombs within the buildings. Satisfied with his tour, his uniform, and his credentials, he finishes his shift, changes his clothes and heads toward Customs in order to retrieve his three crates marked as tourist brochures.

The three crates are the size of storage containers, three feet by four feet by two feet. For the easiest transport, he decides to rent a large SUV—a plain, brown GMC Yukon. He collects his items from his contact there, pays him the usual fee of five thousand dollars and drives directly back to the resort.

Morales tips the bellman twenty Cayman Island dollars and thanks him for helping with the travel-brochure crates. After the bellman leaves, now safely in his room, number 525, he locks the door. Alone in his room, he reviews the layout of the bank in his mind and decides where he will place his devices for maximum impact. Not destructive capability but where they will garner the most attention.

In the morning, he will begin the reconstruction of the bombs and the detonation devices in the three crates. Each will have equal explosive content. The one device will have a little extra special punch with the fuel cell from the Acklins device wrapped in C-4 explosive. It should be a spectacle.

Chapter 29

The sub-bottom sonar registers a hit. "There, right there. See that anomaly?" shouts Jackson. "That's eight feet of metal laying ten feet below the ocean floor. Wait, there's another one. And another. We've got to get down there and excavate that and see what we're dealing with."

"What do you think it is?" Asks Hannah.

"Don't want to get ahead of myself but they're long and have the outline of cannons. If they're bronze, we're onto something big. "

The crew is steadily pulling up loose gold coins, black blobs of silver coins and other jewelry items. They have found two emeralds of different sizes, a gold cross encrusted with emeralds, and a few chains. Ideally, they will find a cannon or the ship's bell; something that is widely accepted as proof of discovery of a specific shipwreck. Jackson is relying on items from John Keating's list on *La Senora de Colon* to tell them if this is the Treasure of Lima.

The thing he can't quite reconcile is the coins' date difference. Over one hundred years difference but no explanation other than that they may be on the site of two different shipwrecks.

Shawn and Paul are on the bottom with the dredging equipment to remove the ten feet of overburden, to see if they have a cannon or two. Removing the overburden is tedious and slow but necessary. Several hours later, from the dredge site, "Holy moly," shouts Paul. "We have a cannon!"

An hour later, they hoist the cannon onto the deck of the *Marauder*. "That's a bronze cannon!" Jackson says excitedly. "Those were utilized by the Spanish until the mid-1700s when most all maritime nations switched to the iron cannons. If this is a bronze cannon, it may not be from our ship. And if that is, in fact, the case, we definitely have another shipwreck here. If it's not *La Senora de Colon*, then it might be the *Nuestra Senora de Madeira* that I learned about in Seville. We just have to keep looking for telltale artifacts including the cannons and the ships bell. Maybe we'll get lucky."

The search continues and the second ping they got from the dredged area is also a cannon, this one iron. Puzzled, Jackson and Shawn research the data files of the archives to determine if the bronze cannon is, in fact, the *Madeira* and now the iron cannon is their ship the *Colon*.

The next day, about one hundred yards from the cannon find, with Ian and George now diving, they get a hit on their metal detectors. As they brush away some of the sediment, they find a rather large iron ring. "Get the sub-bottom sonar down here fast. We've got something that may be an anchor," Ian says to Scotty on deck.

Shawn and Paul lower the sonar down to Ian and George. They run a scan across the area and a very long and narrow iron ping echoes out.

"George, let's get to dredging this. I think we've got an anchor."

The anchor is photographed and analyzed but not disturbed at this point. Back topside, they review the find. "Look here," says Jackson. "The eyehook of the anchor is pointing toward Little Cayman. Meaning the captain secured the anchor to try and steady the ship. The storm pushed the ship northwest. That's where the anchor points. But which ship? Let's keep looking here. There's got to be more. The ship broke apart on a reef that is likely not here anymore and only the remnants of it remain that we see on our dives. If this is where the reef was, there's more treasure here. Let's take a good look at the Keating list of items. Let's also have a look at the computer file of the captain's log from the *Madeira*.

"I think we can safely determine that the coins we're finding dated in the early eighteenth century are from the *Madeira*. And those from the late eighteenth to early nineteenth centuries are from the *Colon*. But we need to keep an eye out for certain items from both. We've found an anchor, a bronze and an iron cannon. I'd love to have a ship's bell or other definitive artifact. Here's what we're specifically looking for from the Keating list and the *Madeira* captain's logbook. First, Keating's list."

Jackson writes down a summary version from the Keating list of items they believe to be on the *Colon*. He reads from the list to the group.

"Two gold relic containers weighing one hundred twenty pounds with six hundred twenty-four topaz, carnelians, emeralds and twelve diamonds. Chalices all coated with gemstones of up to one thousand two hundred and forty-four pieces.

"Chest containing four thousand doubloons of Spanish Marked Eight, one hundred twenty-four swords, five thousand crowns of Mexican Gold, sixty-four daggers, one hundred twenty shoulder belts and twenty-eight round shields. The chest is likely gone and the contents scattered about the bottom.

"Three thousand eight hundred forty cut stones, rings, offering plates and four thousand two hundred sixty-five uncut stones. Same here, they were in a chest, but three hundred years of saltwater, tides and currents will have destroyed that.

"Two candelabra in gold and silver weighing two hundred fifty pounds and one hundred sixty-four rubies.

"Seven-foot solid-gold statue of Virgin Mary with Baby Jesus. It reportedly weighs seven hundred eighty pounds, and has one thousand six hundred eighty-four jewels, including four-inch emeralds, six-inch topazes and seven crosses made of diamonds.

"There is also mention of gold cloth, garments and tapestries but I think we can all agree the ocean has eaten those away.

"And now the *Madeira*, according to the salvaged captain's log that I viewed in Seville. It's a very brief list of what she was carrying. But we've already retrieved a lot of coins.

"The one hundred thousand gold doubloons and two hundred thousand silver coins, along with emeralds and other precious stones. In addition, the mention of a cherished and precious chalice made of hammered gold and adorned with a single ruby in the center of the cup."

"What's our inventory at this point? What have we pulled off the sea floor?" asks Alistair, who had flown in from Nassau with George on the Cessna a few days before.

"We have just over one thousand gold coins, about twice that in silver coin, and ten ornamental rings, fifteen gold necklaces of varying length and size. Also, three emeralds and two daggers. Half of the gold coins are Spanish Marked Eight and half are Mexican Marked Four," Jackson reports reading what they have found and have cross referenced to the list and the diary.

"I'd say that is a successful endeavor. A very nice haul, for sure. I think the Fishers would be proud of our accomplishment," Alistair says. "But, like Jackson, I sure would like to locate a chalice, a sword, an offering plate. I think the coins are just below us in a relatively tight pattern. The relics, they're playing hide-and-seek with us and our equipment."

"Agreed. We'll continue to search. The weather is good for the next week. We're on the treasure so we just keep searching," Jackson confirms.

Back to work they go.

Chapter 30

KABOOM!!! A massive explosion rocks the Ritz Carlton. The fifth floor is the center of the blast. Two floors above and two floors below there is a gaping hole in the side of the resort. A huge black plume of smoke rises and partially obscures the cornflower-blue sky. There are people running from the resort in different directions, including into the ocean. It is a chaotic scene. Sirens can be heard in the background, gradually getting louder as they approach.

Antonio Morales, expert bombmaker, makes an inexcusable oversight concerning the remote detonator on the first bomb. The remote must have been jostled around enough through shipping to be slightly damaged. It causes the activate button on the remote to depress just enough and it sends the detonate signal to the bomb. There were enough explosives, along with the fuel cell for both bombs, to level a medium-sized building. His intent was to have both bombs placed in the bank. One in the stairwell near the vault area and one on the third level where the executive offices are located to adequately garner their attention and deliver his money to Zurich. The plan was to tell the manager that there was a non-existent third, more powerful explosive planted elsewhere in the bank that he would discharge if there was no cooperation with his request.

However, Morales never got to carry out his plan. When he connected the final wire to the bomb in the case, it immediately detonated.

The police and emergency service personnel are busy assisting the injured and unconscious. There are many fatalities. There is a team organizing a field morgue on the grounds of the resort.

The next morning, the *Cayman Compass* headline reads "Cayman Calamity at the Ritz Carlton" in extra-bold lettering. While there is speculation and several theories as to the source and the intent of the bombing, the reporter concludes that there is nothing definitive at this point.

In the days that follow, there is a request from the Cayman Police to the United States ATF National Response Team out of Miami to assist in the investigation of the bombing. The impact of the explosion results in the closing of the resort for a period of several months so the cause of the blast can be determined. The hotel cordons off the damaged section and begins the reconstruction of the rooms, common area, elevators, and the grounds that were damaged from the fallout of the bomb.

All told, five guests, two hotel employees and the occupant of room 525 are listed as fatalities. Several floors of the hotel overlooking the crystal-clear ocean off Seven Mile Beach are destroyed, while others are in various states of disrepair. There would have been many more injuries had the explosion not occurred in the early afternoon when most guests were out of their rooms having lunch, sunbathing or enjoying the sights.

Once the investigation is concluded, the official report is that one individual had assembled a bomb in the room that was detonated for reasons unknown. There is enough DNA evidence to identify Antonia Morales, a Cuban national, as the bomber. There is video showing him assist a bellhop outside the hotel load three containers on a bell cart and enter the elevator. There are no cameras on the guest floors. He is not on any of the terrorist watchlists and is not wanted by any agencies across the globe. The officials conclude that this was not a terrorist attack and that no threats had been issued to the Ritz Carlton. Neither had employees or guests there that day had any ultimatums levied at them. They do not mention that a trace of nuclear material was detected. The final report says that, "after thorough study and analysis of the evidence, the case is closed. No further investigation is necessary.

Unfortunately, the Ritz Carlton on Seven Mile Beach will be closed indefinitely. Crews begin teardowns and rebuilds the following day

Chapter 31

So we agree—tonight, we make our move on the ship, the *Marauder*," Alvarez says. "We'll get our Cigarette to within two hundred yards. Three of us will dive and swim to their boat. We'll board and subdue the crew. I've observed a pattern in the evening that only one or two are on the deck while the others are below deck, either resting or eating or doing whatever they do. The coins and other items are kept in a locker toward the stern. That's our target."

"What if we're seen or met with resistance?" one of the crew asks.

"We obviously retaliate. Return fire and fight. I count six male divers, the old man, two women and the captain. We breach at the stern and port and starboard mid-ship. The three of us will round up the crew and restrain them. We'll contact the Cigarette and have him pull along the stern, where we'll load the gold and silver, take off and make a beeline for Les Cayes. For now, let's prepare our gear and check our weapons and go over the specifics one more time. Then we'll rest until dark."

Meanwhile, on the *Marauder*...

"David, it's great to hear your voice. But normally, you calling gives me pause for caution," Alistair says into the satellite phone.

"Alistair, glad to hear your voice as well. I'm in the Red Sea right now, trying to prevent one country getting scientists from another country to activate a nuclear facility. Sounds worse than it is. We just don't need another hostile country with nuclear arms. So we're doing our duty as always."

"Appreciate you keeping the world a safer place," Alistair responds.

"I do have a small crew in the Caymans that have been keeping watch on you and your treasure hunt there. Only one suspicious vessel to report. It's a forty-two foot Auroris Cigarette. Been watching from a distance. They aren't pretending to fish or dive or anything. Just watching."

"We've noticed a lot of curiosity seekers hanging about but they don't stay for very long and it's always different boats," Alistair informs David.

"Our drone hasn't detected anything that would suggest foul play, but my gut tells me you should be observant."

David provides Alistair with a detailed description of the boat and the crew on board. "We haven't observed anything unusual in terms of weapons of any kind but that doesn't mean they aren't stored somewhere in the forward cabin. You know the drill, Alistair. Head on a swivel."

"Yes, David, I'll make sure we're on our toes and that the crew is informed and on guard. Thanks, as always. Now go save the world again." Alistair chuckles.

"I'm doing what I can. Won't be long till I'll be living a life of leisure like you, my friend." David laughs out loud. "See you at the Victoria!"

And with that, the call ends.

Chapter 32

Alistair receives a call from the Division of Historical Resources and the Department of the Environment on Grand Cayman. They are coming the day after tomorrow to observe the site and see if they are being good stewards of the land and sea. This, in large part, will determine if the Cayman government will renew their dredging permit, which expires in forty-five days. They also ask him to provide a list of the items found through their efforts to date.

"I've found something! This is a new item under the sea floor. Just about five feet below. It's shaped like a bell," Jackson reports over the comm system.

"That's fantastic," Ian responds from the ship. "When do you want to dredge and excavate it?"

"I'd love to do it now but the currents are running pretty swift today and visibility is getting poor. I'd rather wait and see if we have better conditions in a day or two, to be honest."

Ian replies to Jackson, "You coming up now?"

"Give me another twenty minutes. I've still got good air and I want to run the metal detectors over the area and run the sub-bottom scanner one more time around this area of the grid. Then, when we resume dredging this section we will know precisely where we want to dig." Jackson calls out.

"See you in twenty then. I'll be here monitoring you until you surface," Ian responds.

Thirty minutes later, Jackson has removed his gear but remains in his jet-black wetsuit. "I had a couple of hits down there of even stranger-shaped items. Some large, some not. But I need to look at the readout of the scans. I also had some more hits for coins with the metal detector. I wouldn't say we're on the motherlode, but we're certainly on the trail."

"We've got the Cayman government sending some reps for observation and to review our list of items we've retrieved," Alistair informs the group. "I'm sure part of their visit is to estimate their agreed-to commission. And to make sure we're not endangering the reef, the amateur dive sites and the waters around the island. I've explained that, if they wished, we would fill in and restore any dredged areas for conservation purposes. They said they would let us know how to proceed with any reclamation."

"I've sent our documentation and photos of the bronze and iron cannons to a friend of mine who's an expert in armaments of the sixteenth through nineteenth centuries. I'm waiting to hear from him. But in my humble opinion, the bronze cannon is from the *Nuestra Senora de Madeira*, from the early eighteenth century," Jackson tells the team.

Hannah speaks up: "Why did some of the ships have bronze cannons and some have iron cannons?"

"Excellent question, Hannah," Jackson answers. "Ships can only carry a certain amount of weight without risking sinking or capsizing. Bronze is lighter than iron. Therefore, a Spanish galleon could carry many more cannons made of bronze than if they used iron. So, more cannons for the same weight. Also, the Spanish loved to intricately decorate their ships, and this included their cannons. Bronze was a much better medium for adorning their cannons' various relief designs, many particular to the specific ship they were sailing. Also, early on, iron cannons had a tendency to explode and were initially less accurate than those made of bronze. And bronze became more expensive and used as material for other items of the day. As the iron cannons developed, while much heavier, they produced more accuracy and distance, and became the material of choice until other metals, such as brass and steel, became popular."

The group talks about their successes so far and they discuss the possibilities, knowing that Jackson has found several more anomalies right below them. The discussion carries on into the early evening until twilight settles in around them.

Just off their port side, a forty-two-foot Auroris Cigarette begins slowly moving for the *Marauder*. It quietly drops anchor at two hundred yards and settles quietly in place on a very calm sea. The three men in wetsuits pack their tools, including their walkie-talkies and handguns, into dry bags and strap them to their backs.

Slowly and steadily, the trio take their positions around the ship. The water is dark and there are no underwater lights running. Silence on deck. No movement. Alvarez climbs silently aboard from the stern at the swim platform. He then secures a rope to the rail on the port and the starboard side and quietly lowers the rope into the water. The other two team members slowly scale the side of the ship, making no noise at all. There is barely a whisper of wind on the water. The three, now on board the

Marauder, inch their way toward the wheelhouse from three different angles. The only sound is the dripping noise as water slides off their wetsuits onto the deck. Muffled conversation below deck. Occasional laughter. The men slowly make their way to the door leading to the galley.

Suddenly, they hear steps coming up the ladder from below and a woman's voice saying, "I left it on deck. I'll go grab it."

As Sandra opens the door, she is met with a strong arm around her waist and a firm hand across her mouth. She emits a groan of surprise as Alvarez's arm compresses across her stomach and he whispers into her ear, "Quiet. We're not going to harm you or the others if you do as I say."

Below deck, Shawn says, "Did you hear something? Like a groan or a soft moan?" The rest of the crew acknowledge not hearing anything. Shawn goes to his berth and recovers the trusty Glock 9mm that has been at his side for many years. Without speaking, Scotty and Paul also retrieve and ready their sidearms. Shawn looks at George, who has already drawn his pistol and motions Alistair to stay put below deck. Scotty motions to Richard to also stay below deck and hands him a sidearm for their protection. Ian and Hannah come out of their small cabin, and Ian whispers, "What's going on?"

"Sandra went up to grab one of the notebooks that we left on deck and I heard a sound, as if she were being forcibly subdued. We're going to see what's going on," Shawn says softly.

"I'll grab my 9mm. I'll be right behind you. Hannah, you stay put," Ian says.

On deck, Alvarez keeps a tight grip on Sandra. He motions the other two pirates to go below deck. They, too, have drawn their pistols from their dry bags. They open the door and are greeted by the five resolute men in single file ascending the stairs. One of the boarding pirates fires and all hell breaks loose in the stairwell. The first pirate is shot by

Scotty, who is up front. The pirate goes down. The second pirate fires two rounds into the stairwell and Shawn and Paul go down. George fires and drops the second pirate.

"Stop or I'll kill this young lady!" Alvarez shouts from outside the stairwell. There is no response. George motions to Ian to go through the galley and get topside from the rear ladder. "They think they have us pinned down. Circle around and take any others on deck out of the picture. I can keep the one outside the stairwell occupied. I'll tell him not to harm Sandra or he'll soon know what hell is."

Ian circles around with Richard, who trails behind by a few yards. Ian emerges and quietly moves toward the sound of George and the other pirate talking back and forth. Apparently, there are no other perpetrators on board. Alvarez threatens to harm Sandra if he isn't given the gold coin and allowed to go free. George informs him that it isn't going to be his day. Ian takes aim at the back of

Alvarez's. He holds steady since Sandra isn't out of his line of fire.

As if on cue, Sandra stomps on Alvarez's foot, just hard enough that her head and shoulders bow away from him.

Then Ian fires.

Alvarez drops Sandra, then falls to the deck. Just off the port side of the *Marauder*, the Cigarette boat is boarded and the pilot is taken into custody by a small group of men from a boat that has been observing the entire scene.

Both boats, now captained by David Smith's surveillance team, head toward the dock at Cayman Brac.

Before leaving, the captain swings close to the *Marauder*. "We'll be needing to clean up the mess from your uninvited guests."

The stairwell is blocked. Scotty has been shot in the neck and is prepped for transport to the medical center on Cayman Brac. Shawn has been shot in the shoulder. The bullet passed through, missing his major organs, but hit Paul in the side. Paul was also hit with a second bullet from the assailant in his sternum. He lays motionless, his body lifeless. Everyone on the Marauder is in shock over the loss of Paul.

"Wait, Ian says, I think we should at least take a moment to honor Paul and his sacrifice to this group. I'll start." Ian says a few words about their experience and the selflessness Paul gave throughout the operation. Then Shawn speaks about what a great diver and searcher Paul was. Jackson echoes Shawn's sentiments. Alistair provides the final thoughts on Paul and his contributions. Then entire group bowed their heads in silent gratitude. One of the crew members on the Pursuit raises his rifle and fires three times. After the brief memorial, Paul's body is transferred to the Pursuit 428C.

"We'll take care of Paul and your three intruders. You take care of the others." As the Smith team prepares to depart, he says to Alistair, "Mr. Smith sends his regards."

Chapter 33

Shawn returns the following day with his arm in a sling and with a generous dose of pain relievers from the medical center on Cayman Brac. Scotty has to undergo surgery to remove the bullet and repair the damage done to his neck area. The prognosis is good for him to fully recover. David Smith makes arrangements to have Scotty transferred to Mount Sinai Medical Center in Miami for further recovery.

The following day, around noon, the Cayman Islands Division of Historical Resources and the Department of the Environment representatives pay a visit to the dive site. Jackson reviews the log of the recovered items with them and provides them with a copy of the findings thus far. He explains that the two different cannons found represent two different shipwrecks. He has had an expert review the cannons in detail and that is the conclusion. "We are certain the bronze cannon is from the *Nuestra*

Senora de Madeira, from 1730. The iron cannon is believed to be from the wreck of *La Senora de Colon*, around 1820. You'll notice the dates and mints of the coins support this theory. We're searching for a bell, or something to identify her definitively."

Alistair takes the group to a sitting area toward the stern and shows them a live ROV feed. "I wanted to show you the area we're currently dredging, where the cannons were found. As you can see, we've done an excellent job of not disturbing the neighboring reef. And, as I said on the phone a few days ago, if you wish, we will backfill those dredged areas with the displaced material."

A few hours later, they bid farewell to their government contacts, assured that they will be able to dredge the additional forty-two days based on the original permits. Any extension or renewal of the permits can be decided then. Alistair and Jackson do not get a good feeling about the permits being renewed or extended.

"Let's get back to the bottom. We're three men down, so extend your dives as long as you can. Let's find as much as possible in the next forty-two days in case we can't continue."

"Let's get to it," Alistair says.

"Shawn, can you manage the comms with your bad shoulder?" Jackson asks.

"I can do that," Shawn responds. "And don't forget, Sandra is an experienced diver. Put a wet suit on her and give her a metal detector."

With that, the team resumes diving on the site of the bell-shaped anomaly as well as the other hits from Jackson's last dive.

Three days later...

"There she is. That's what we've been looking for," Jackson exclaims from the seafloor forty feet below. "It's a bell. Let me loosen the sand and rock around it, and I'll try to free it. Drop down three or four straps, please. Once I get it loose, I'll secure its ascension to the ship."

"Roger that," Shawn replies.

Hannah, Sandra and Ian are in charge of sending and retrieving items from the wreck. Jackson, Ian, Sandra, George and Alistair are the divers. Richard is the captain for the *Marauder* and jumps on the dive boat when needed.

An hour later, the bell makes it way to the deck of the *Marauder*. There is encrustation to be removed but there, across the bell, it says: *La Senora de Colon*. This confirms that Jackson was correct all along. The Treasure of Lima was not buried or lost in the Pacific Ocean near Cocos Island. It was rerouted and sent from Panama to Savannah until a hurricane sent the treasure down here, off the coast of Cayman Brac.

With his good hand, Shawn grabs Jackson's shoulder and says, "Great job, my friend. No one, including me, believed you at the start, but here is the bell.

And the iron cannon will be from the same ship. Congratulations!"

"We did find the ship's bell and we did find the cannon and we have found thousands of coins. It is a great haul and a great discovery," Jackson says. "I sure would like to find something off Keating's list that tells me this is the final resting place for her.

"Chin up! We still have thirty-plus days under the permits. Let's just keep looking. If there are items from that list here, we'll find them," Shawn reassures Jackson.

They toil away for another two weeks and find two chalices: one bejeweled and one made of hammered gold with one ruby. They find hundreds more gold coins.

Then, a few days later, Sandra and Ian are excavating an area where several metallic hits have been made. They spend a great deal of the morning getting down to the suspected depth. And then, "Oh, my God!" Ian yells.

"What have you got?" Alistair asks over the comm system.

"It's the face of a woman in gold, life-size. Let me get some of this overburden cleared around her."

Ian and Sandra continue clearing. "It's a gold statue. She's laying at a thirty-degree angle in the sand so it will take some more excavating—and she's holding a baby. There are jewels and some crosses with what looks like diamonds encrusted on them. It's the statue of Mary and Jesus that's on the manifest. It really is the Treasure of Lima!" Sandra yells.

As the days go by, more and more artifacts from Keating's list emerge from the seafloor, feeling human touch and seeing light for the first time in over two hundred years.

Alistair, Jackson and Shawn catalog and reference GPS coordinates on everything that is found, including depth and condition. They also document the dredging and excavation done to remove the relics from the seafloor.

Alistair begins making arrangements to have the treasure tightly secured on land until they can get it to a proper destination.

Alistair and Jackson discuss where and how to divide the spoils. "None of these items would have been found if you hadn't solved the riddle of how the treasure came to rest here in the Caribbean," Alistair says to Jackson.

"And none of this would have been found so quickly without you being so generous in obtaining and providing the equipment to get us to the treasure," Jackson replies. "We owe the Cayman Islands their fee for the rights. Let's take that off the top. I recommend that we then pay expenses for the equipment, the transport costs, travel fees and similar items."

"I don't need to be reimbursed, Jackson," Alistair says.

"I insist on some recompense," Jackson insists.

They go back and forth with offer and counteroffer and, finally, Alistair agrees to a stated amount that Jackson says he must take. "That leaves us with a fairly hefty amount to divide equally among the team. I'd like for Paul's family to get an equal share as well."

"I'd like to create an exhibit, if you don't mind, that we can lend to maritime museums around the world, so they may witness the Treasure of Lima firsthand. Eventually, we should house the display permanently in Seville, Spain. The General Archive of the Indies in the ancient merchants' exchange would be ideal. We can charge a fee for loaning the artifacts, which will cover the expense of moving and securing them at each location."

"I'm in favor," Jackson agrees.

Twenty-five days later, the Cayman government informs Alistair that their permits will not be renewed. The Division of Historical Resources and the Department of the Environment have decided to secure the dive site for historical significance and plan to make it a boost to their tourism industry.

Alistair tells Jackson they can sell the boats and any of the search equipment. The sub-bottom sonar will be returned to the Seafarer search group along with a donation for the rental equipment.

And as a parting gift to the friendly people of Cayman Brac, for their help and hospitality, two Ben Burns Power Stations are set up for the community. Alistair trains several of the islanders on their use and maintenance. He's confident this, too, is a worthy placement of their device and will help the people there.

Chapter 34

This is the end of the adventure for our group. Alistair will continue to work on the floating platforms as a secondary measure. They will be practical to set up and serve as housing after waterborne disasters such as hurricanes, tsunamis and the like. However, Alistair and the team vow to redirect their efforts and dedicate their resources to the development of the Ben Burns Power Station, placing them in poverty-stricken areas, or areas of extreme isolation, in order to provide power and clean water. The power provided by the units will give people a way of life they could previously not have imagined. As part of placement of the Ben Burns Power Station—also known as the BBPS—Alistair and Virgin Power and Water have created a division of agriculture. Once the units are placed, members from the division will embed with the locals and show them how to properly grow plants and herbs and irrigate with the unit. In addition, a startup power division has been created to show the villagers and locals how to use and distribute power to increase their quality of life.

This is all made possible with Emma's pipeline innovation. The unit still runs on seawater. But now the unit can be installed away from the source of seawater, then run through one set of pipes to the inland location of the BBPS. The seawater is then piped to the BBPS so the unit runs just like the prototype units, placed near the water source. The by-product of clean drinking water is collected and distributed through an irrigation system for agriculture or stored in large water containers for drinking. It's not the last version of the pipeline but it is functional now.

Emma tells the group, "With great leadership from Jean Pierre, we decided it would be best to run the pipeline to Belladere through the Dominican Republic side. Jean Pierre didn't want to deal with the corrupt government of Haiti. So, we installed a

BBPS at Pedernales, Jimaní and Comendador in exchange for the right of way in each town to Belladere."

The city of Pedernales is the capital of the Pedernales Province in the Dominican Republic. Jimaní is the capital of the Independent Province of the Dominican Republic. It is a main border crossing into Haiti. Comendador is adjacent to Jean's village or Belladere.

Jean Pierre and his small band of rebels start a revolution in his native land. Not to overthrow the government or harm anyone. He kept true to his vision to help his people.

The James team, with their device and their simple pipeline system, proved to be invaluable to Jean's efforts to provide resources for the villagers so they could not only survive, but prosper. The effort took almost a year and it also required the cooperation of his Dominican neighbors just across the border. The villages being serviced by the power devices are small enough that big government officials pay them no attention whatsoever. In fact, they are certain those officials have no idea they even exist. It allows the people the time to not only utilize the power and water from the devices, but also to learn techniques to thrive in their land.

Jean Pierre and Paul Baptiste work with agriculture team and the power team from Virgin Power and Water. They educate and tutor the people in farming techniques that will protect the topsoil, increase the crop yields and prevent flooding. The power sources allow people to light their homes, and provide the power needed for cooking, farming and maintaining their land.

Jean begins to realize the recognition that he deserves from the people for his efforts to be a peaceful difference maker. His is given the nickname "Peace Rebel," which he readily accepts.

Libérer Haiti develops a school for the children of the area, to educate them not only in farming and being keepers of their land but, with encouragement and assistance from Foxy Caldwell, to teach basic skills like math, science and reading. Foxy developed, and now runs, a school on Jost Van Dyke to help his island's children. They have also developed a learning center for the adults who wish to learn these same skills.

There are plans for a small medical center that will focus on the health and wellbeing of people on both sides of the border. They will provide classes in hygiene, sanitation and maintaining a proper health regime.

Asked if he's worried about the Haitian government interfering with his efforts or trying to commandeer the village's Ben Burns Power Station, he says, "No. I don't think our leaders could find us on a map." What he didn't say was that he has developed some very important connections with this endeavor who have assured him that, if he senses imminent threats, he should let them know immediately and they will muster the assistance and the protection he might require. His efforts and the work with Virgin Power and Water and the Alistair James team significantly improve the circumstances of him and his people, as well as the lives of those on the other side of the border who are continuing to assist him. In addition, the James team and Virgin are making this effort a model for implementing the inland Ben Burns Power Stations for other needy areas.

Jean Pierre, by resisting the temptation presented by Antonio Morales, has achieved great success in his efforts to lead a peaceful and powerful revolution.

Chapter 35

Alistair reflects back over the adventure they've had, never thinking that the development of the power station would have brought them full circle to the intended use of the unit. To help the less fortunate and the underserved by providing free power and water. He takes a deep breath and then exhales slowly with a deep sense of satisfaction.

They have rooms for a few days at the Cayman Brac resort, in order to enjoy some comfort and try to rid themselves of their sea legs. They all gather in the dining area to enjoy a group dinner before going their separate ways on the following day.

"Alistair, you, Emma, Ethan, Aiden, George and, of course, Benjamin, have changed the world for the better." Ian smiles as he shakes Alistair's hand and then embraces him. "We're all proud to have played a role, no matter how small, in seeing this come to fruition. I'm sorry that Benjamin is no longer with us, but his sacrifice, and that of Paul, will certainly not be forgotten."

"I can't believe they're gone," Alistair says as he wipes a tear from his right eye. I've set up memorial scholarships in each of their hometowns for students wishing to pursue the sciences. Their memories will live on as long as I do. So, what now? What will you do?"

"Hannah and I are going to be beach bums. But we've also decided we'll set up a charter for the kids of the Virgin Islands. We'll teach them all about their home and the sea, and how to continue to be good stewards of the land with which they've been blessed. And I expect that they'll teach us a thing or two as well," Ian explains.

"Sandra and I are going to travel," Shawn says. We're going by boat, plane and train. First, the United States and the places we've always wanted to see. Then we'll work our way around the globe. Australia, New Zealand, Japan, Vietnam and across

Asia. Backpacking through Europe. All of it. We have nothing to keep us in one place and, thanks to you—and the treasure—we have no financial worries. Once we complete that adventure, we'll have a cocktail and decide what's next. Ian and Hannah will have the *Second Wind* in St. John and have given us an open invitation to visit from time to time. And I'm going to put the *Migration* back at Bud N' Mary's Marina in Islamorada, giving us a floating condo there when we need it."

"And you all always have a place to stay should you make your way to jolly old England," Alistair says with a smile.

"I'm going to look for the next treasure. You know, they still haven't found Blackbeard's treasure!" Jackson says with a laugh. The others laugh with him. "And I'm going to document the method of discovery we used to be minimally invasive to the ocean and the reefs while still successful in uncovering the treasure."

Alistair addresses the group with a toast of thanks and a request: "Please, once again, accept my thanks and my appreciation for each and every one of you. When this adventure began several years back in that sleepy coastal town in America, I couldn't comprehend the dangers, the adventures and the successes we would have. Neither could I have imagined meeting and becoming lifelong friends with a group such as yourselves. We have had ourselves quite the journey. I couldn't ask for any more than that. Here's to us, and here's to the memory of Benjamin and Paul."

Alistair raises his glass and the rest of the group raise theirs as well as Alistair says, "To Benjamin and to Paul, long live their memory and their contributions to us all."

After a moment of quiet reflection and few brief comments from the group, Ian turns to Alistair and quietly says with a smile, "Alistair, I wouldn't trade it for the world. However, I do hope our days of getting shot at, injured, kidnapped and chased are over."

Alistair laughs and says, "I couldn't agree more, Ian." He continues, "There is one more thing I'd like you all to do for me," Alistair says. "Before you go on your new journeys, I would appreciate your accompanying me to London for the first exhibition of our Cayman cache. Then we can say our teary goodbyes and be on our way."

Everyone enthusiastically accepts. Ian says, "And as I've told Shawn before, we say 'see you later,' Alistair. Goodbyes are permanent."

Epilogue

The president of the National Maritime Museum is happily greeting guests for the presentation of their most prized possession, as well as other artifacts recovered and recently loaned to the institution for the initial display. The National Maritime Museum is located in Greenwich, London. The museum formally opened on 27 April 1937 under King George VI.

Greenwich itself is steeped in its association with the sea. It was a landing place for the Romans, Henry VIII lived there, the Royal Navy has roots on the waterfront, and Charles II founded the Royal Observatory in 1675 for "finding the longitude of places." The home of Greenwich Mean Time and the Prime Meridian since 1884. Navigators across the world set their clocks according to its time of day. The museum contains over two million items detailing the history of Britain at sea including maritime art, British and Dutch, cartography and manuscripts, including official public records, ship models and plans, scientific and navigational instruments, and instruments for time-keeping and astronomy.

Alistair and George look dashing standing in the hall that houses the treasure. In the center is the final relic to be revealed. Alistair is near a spot in the room surrounded by the museum's dignitaries along with honored guests. George seems edgy, his eyes darting left to right, wary of anything out of the ordinary. Ever protective and ever aware, George leaves nothing to chance. The other members of the treasure group are not far behind, including Jackson, Ian, Shawn, Sandra, Hannah, Scotty and Richard. There are two wreaths for the missing, Benjamin and Paul. Shawn with his left arm in a sling. Scotty in a wheelchair, still recovering from injuries. Emma holding Alistair's arm. Ethan and Aiden with their wives.

The National Maritime Museum's president takes center podium and raises his hand to quiet the guests. "Thank you so much for attending. We are very excited to be the first to present to the world an incredible recovery of invaluable relics. They are on loan to us for the next several months. Thank you to Alistair James and his crew for recovering and safeguarding these exquisite and important artifacts." The president gestures with his outstretched arms to the artifacts from the treasure strategically placed about the perimeter of the grand room.

The ship's bell from the galleon that Thompson and Forbes loaded the treasure onto for their journey toward Savannah harbor. *La Senora de Colon* emblazoned on the bell. Also on display are items from John Keating's inventory of the treasure trove, including three bejeweled chalices, several swords, a solid-gold candelabra, a display case of the loose jewels found including the topaz, carnelians, emeralds, rubies and diamonds. Several display cases with gold coin and silver in various states, from black blob in seawater to totally restored coins. There are miscellaneous chains, necklaces and rings encased in glass displays.

A standing ovation and polite applause from the gathering of dignitaries ensues. Alistair waves his hand to the crowd in acknowledgement. He stands beside the cloaked object. He gently grasps the cord to reveal what is underneath. With a subtle pull, the velvet cloak falls to the ground. The audience gasps in astonishment and awe. Standing before them, and next to Alistair, is a gleaming seven-foot solid-gold statue of the Virgin Mary with Baby Jesus rolled on her gold chasuble adorned with one thousand six hundred eighty-four jewels, including four-inch emeralds, six-inch topazes and seven crosses made of diamonds.

"I give to you the statue of the Virgin Mary and the Baby Jesus. It was one of the recoveries made from the wreck that transported the Treasure of Lima in

1820," Alistair states proudly. "Possibly one of the most important finds in recent history."

Further murmuring in the crowd. Questions from the group surrounding the statue are directed at Alistair regarding the who, what, when and where of the find.

"Where did you locate the wreck?"

"What led you to that location?"

"How long did you have to search and dredge?"

Alistair answers all questions patiently and succinctly. After the questions cease, the crowd is allowed a closer inspection, but outside the velvet ropes surrounding the artifact.

As the crowd continues to murmur in amazement at the statue and the collection, Ian leans in to ask quietly of Alistair, "Whatever became of the other chalice? The hammered-gold one with the single ruby? I don't see it on display."

"I wondered why the captain would mention it in his diary but there is no mention of it in the logbook. He was told by the priests that it could be the Holy Grail, the Cup of Christ," Alistair says. "I'm not saying it is or it isn't. I really did want to include it in the small exhibit we created for the *Nuestra Senora de Madeira*. But I'm unsure. How would the world react? Would it receive the reverence and respect such a priceless item truly deserves? Would religious leaders or nations fight over possessing it? Would others disparage its authenticity? I pondered that decision long and hard. Then I took it upon myself to gift it to someone who would use it properly and not subject it to the scrutiny of the world."

In a small Catholic church on Cayman Brac...

A priest holds a chalice and wipes it with a clean cloth. The chalice and the offering plate are a gift from an older, English gentleman, from the treasure hunters who raised the items off the ocean floor. He is grateful for the gift to his small church. The young priest, having concluded his service for his small congregation, places the chalice in a case and stores it with the other sacraments from mass inside the altar. He feels a special calm and happiness today. It's another glorious day here on Cayman Brac.

The End

About the Author...

Jeff Thompson is a retired insurance industry manager and later sales representative. He currently resides in the Grand Strand of South Carolina. This is his fourth novel in the Ian Marshall series. He also authored the Mischief Macaw children's book series. Visit his website, **www.papatbooks.com**, for more information and further adventures.

Made in the USA
Middletown, DE
01 June 2025

76236971R00167